BULLSEYE BRIDE

BOOKS BY KARI TRUMBO

Historical:

The Belle Fourche Chronicles

Wherever the Road will Lead
To a Brighter Tomorrow
Valley of Promise
Battle for Her Heart
Belle Fourche Legacy

Regional Romance

Black Hills Song
Great Lakes Light

Brothers of Belle Fourche

Teach me to Love
What the Heart Holds
Deep Longing of the Soul
Saved by Grace
When Shadows Break
A Lady Loves Much

And many more!

ALSO BY KARI TRUMBO

Contemporary:

Wayside Ranch

Operation: Restoration

Operation: Return

Operation: Chosen

More coming soon!

Dawson's Valley

Hometown Hero

Sweet Temptation

Love's Security

Single titles

Deadly Yellowstone Secrets

(Love Inspired Suspense)

And many more!

BULLSEYE Bride

BY

KARI TRUMBO

the Pink Pistol SISTERHOOD

BOOK 5

Bullseye Bride
ISBN: 9798393219024
Copyright © 2023 by Kari Trumbo
Published by Inked in Faith Publications LLC
Printed in the United States of America
All rights reserved.

Excerpt from:
Love on Target (Pink Pistol Sisterhood Series) by Shanna Hatfield
Copyright (c) 2023 Shanna Hatfield

Scripture quotations are from the King James Version of the Bible. No part of this book may be reproduced in any form or by any electronic or mechanical means, including information storage and retrieval systems, without written permission from the author, except for the use of brief quotations in a book review.
This is a work of fiction. Names, dates, places, and situations are all products of the author's imagination and should not be construed as real. Any resemblance to real persons, places, or events is unintended and accidental.
Cover design by Shanna Hatfield.
Editing: Elizabeth Lance

I am so thankful to be a part of not only this group of ladies writing together in this series, but the entire group of bloggers and authors at the Petticoats & Pistols blog. Without them, this series wouldn't have happened and all these friendships wouldn't be as deep or as endearing. Thank you, ladies. You are treasures.

1

A shiver ran up Kitty's spine as she touched the cloudy glass of the pawnshop's front window. Beyond it, barely visible, was a dark wooden case with the items that would be available for sale in one week if the owner didn't pay back his loan. Even though she had only one dollar to her name, she wanted what was in that wooden case more than almost anything.

She shook the desire from her shoulders and straightened her spine. How childish. She should want her father's return more than the beautiful pearl-handled pistol nestled within the green velvet–lined wooden box. He'd been gone for over two months, and Ma speculated he was dead—not that his loss seemed to change her day much.

Other than the fact that they couldn't pay to live in their house.

Kitty's threadbare coat, borrowed from Ma, did

little to keep out the chill of the wind blowing over the Black Hills and down into Deadwood Gulch. Spring was on the way, but not quite there yet. Summer would mean she could hunt more easily and they wouldn't need so much wood for the stove. Her four brothers were a big help, but without Pa there to provide, their storage of store-bought staples was gone. No money left for a pink pistol, no matter how pretty it might be.

No, her pocket held just enough to enter the Deadwood Annual Shooting Contest. Thad Easton's printed poster hung inside the window, just out of the way enough to still see the goods on the shelves. That fact mattered little because she knew what the sheet said by heart. The competition was in fourteen days, and she hadn't signed up yet. Mainly because she'd had to find the time to do odd jobs around town until she'd earned the highly expensive entry fee of a whole dollar.

Kitty clenched her fist and reached for the door just as a large masculine hand did the same. It brushed across hers, making her shiver slightly and jump. Where had he come from? Looking up, her vision caught and held on the man she'd just been thinking about. Thad Easton smiled at her and held the door open.

"Katherine, good to see you in town."

She swallowed hard. How was she to reply to that? She only came into town to go to church and to sell the pelts of the rabbits and other small animals she caught for food around their house, though the few pennies those sales brought in were barely enough to buy flour. "Good to see you, too." She swallowed hard again. The man was far too handsome, and wealthy, for her to go all doe-eyed, but her heart raced all the same.

Her words made Thad's smile grow even more. "Are you here to sign up for the contest? None of the other ladies will bother if you don't. There is no competition without you."

He'd noticed? Warmth spread over her cheeks as she ducked in the door and out of the street.

"Now, Thad, don't you let your words go to Kitty's head. That sheriff's wife from over in Belle Fourche has already signed up, and I hear she's a crack shot," Dalton said.

Kitty rushed to the front of the shop to look at the signup sheet. Sure enough, her friend Hannah Longfellow had signed up to compete. Hannah had teased her husband, Blake, for years about driving a car wherever he needed to go instead of riding a horse, but that very thing allowed Hannah to have friends in other towns.

"I couldn't compete against Hannah." Kitty bit her lip. Well, she could, but she wouldn't want to. Especially since there was no prize for the women's competition. Hannah was her closest friend, and the shot was a measly thirty yards. Barely a challenge.

"You mean you're not going to enter?" Dalton, the pawnbroker, leaned over the counter and smacked his lips, shoving his wad of tobacco deeper into his cheek with his tongue. "You out of money, ain't ya?" Greed narrowed his eyes. "I'm sure we could find something in that hovel worth the dollar entry fee."

Thad held up his hand. "Dalton, don't put words in her mouth or start taking an inventory of her goods before she needs your unique…services." His lip curled, making Kitty wonder why he'd put the signup only in the pawn shop if he didn't want to come in here.

"Maybe you have some money?" Dalton poked her arm hard enough to shove her back into Thad, who righted her immediately, but not before the flutters in her stomach had taken flight. Dalton growled like she'd moved intentionally and pushed the sheet toward her. "I don't think Mrs. Longfellow would mind a little friendly competition."

Kitty took a step back away from the counter and Dalton's poking finger. "Honestly, I only came in to look more closely at the pistol in the window. Mine has seen better days." Not that she could replace it. Ma had warned her if she didn't win the elite shooting competition, they would have to go live with Pa's brother, Damion Horwath—their only living relative. Ma was purposely hiding their situation from Damion for as long as possible, but he would find out about Pa soon enough.

"That pistol ain't for sale just yet. The owner was in need of ticket money to get to Texas. He promised he'd be back in time to claim it. His date isn't up for two whole days yet." Dalton snickered. "If you have money, might as well put it to good use. That dollar will help fund the—" He stopped talking as she held up her hand.

"I can read the sign," Kitty said. Though Dalton probably assumed she couldn't. She stored away the information on the exact date the pistol would be available for later. The cost was beyond what she could afford anyway, especially with the entry fee that had to be paid or she would lose everything. "Why are there never any women in the elite competition?" she asked. If they wanted her to join the women's so badly, why couldn't she shoot against the men instead and win the prize money needed to save her family?

"A woman?" Dalton laughed and slapped the counter so loudly Kitty jumped. "You think a woman could beat out Thad or Amos? Not likely. Those two bring all the money. Every year we wait to see who's a better shot."

Thad flattened his lips. "Or to see which shooter the wind favors that year. I think Amos and I are equally matched. Maybe adding in a new contender would bring about a little excitement. It couldn't hurt. The project from the proceeds is huge this year. We need all the entries we can get."

Dalton snorted and tugged the sheet out of reach. "But not by contending against a woman. There's no way to win that. Either the man will claim he let her win to honor her or to save face, *or* they would just drop out of the running and refuse to compete. I can promise you, put a woman's name on that elite shooter list and no one will come because they'll assume there won't be a contest at all." He slammed his finger down on the entry sheet for good measure.

Kitty tried to school her features and prayed neither man could read on her face how she felt. Dalton could just as well have punched her. Without that money, her home and her freedom were gone. She raced for the door before either man could see her tears. In a blur, she took in the shiny wooden box and beautiful pearl-handled pistol once more. It would never be hers.

THAD WATCHED Katherine race from the pawnshop, dash past the window, and disappear out of sight.

"It ain't right, Thad. That girl shouldn't have to hunt to provide food for that family," Dalton said, his tone changing to one of worry.

Thad swallowed the acrid words that wanted to burst forth. Dalton had been downright cruel to the girl he apparently felt sorry for. "She can't help that her father is a treacherous heathen who cheated the snake trappers near the Badlands."

Dalton winced, showing large gaps of missing teeth. "I hadn't heard what happened to him. How do you know?"

"I don't. I just heard him bragging as he was waiting for his missus outside of church right before he disappeared. He said he was going to the Badlands to skunk a few skunks. Since he hasn't returned yet, I would assume they had the same idea and caught up with him first."

"That leaves Mrs. Horwath in a bad place. Five kids, not that Kitty's a child anymore."

No, she certainly wasn't. Kitty's pink cheeks and lovely blonde hair made her very appealing to look at, but her quick wit, precise aim with a pistol, and her father's standing in the community made her an unacceptable mate for most men who were either looking for no more attachment than a sporting gal or had money and were looking for a gentle woman to escape the rough edges of Deadwood in their homes.

While Thad was of the latter set himself, he hadn't found any of the few wealthy ladies in town to suit him. Their fathers had invited him out for cigars and wanted to know all about his lumber investments, but knowing what they were about, he offered little information. The dealings with these fathers felt no deeper than picking a cow for butchering. If they didn't know what his affairs were like, then they couldn't pester him as much.

"That pistol she was talking about… It truly is unique. I'm not surprised it caught her eye," Thad said. He strode toward the case, and Dalton followed on his heels like a starving dog. Dalton licked his lips, accentuating the vision.

"It is. I think those are genuine pearl handles. Very rare to see anything like them. And that case, very well made. I'm sure I'll get more for it than I lent."

Thad eyed the unscrupulous man. "After two more days."

"Of course." Dalton squirmed slightly, then backed away a few paces. "I'm an honest man, Thad. You know that."

Thad kept his feelings to himself, as he tried to often do. "Who else is signed up for the contest? It's only two weeks away, and the need for the roller rink is great. There's only so much I can donate as far as the cost of lumber. I have to pay my men."

Dalton whistled through his teeth. "Not great enough to have women shooting more than they already are. I know Kitty was the one who argued with Slade to get a women's division in the first place, but that's not why people come."

"You don't think so? Slade didn't want to then, but he's glad he made the exception now."

"Don't you dare let her sign up and put all my hard work of rounding people up go to waste. If you want everyone but the women to drop out, you let her sign up. And while you're at it, you'd best go borrow the dunce cap from the school because people will be laughing at you up one side of the street and down the other. They'll remember you for generations as the one who slowed down progress in Deadwood. And let's face it, progress is pretty slow as it is."

Thad couldn't deny it. So many people wanted Deadwood to stay rough and tumble. Judging by Dalton's immediate reaction, he felt so, too. Life wasn't fair, and this situation was particularly unfair. Unlike any of the other contestants, himself most of all, Katherine needed the money so that her family could buy foodstuffs and necessities. Her coat had looked more thread than fabric. Winning might not save them, but it would go a long way toward helping the whole family get back on their feet.

"I'm not making any decision like that without Mr. Slade. So don't get your dander up." Thad adjusted his hat, ready to head back to work.

Dalton nodded and tapped the tip of his pencil on the paper. "She still didn't sign up for the women's contest. You don't think she's so bad off that she won't?"

Thad didn't answer right away. Despite what Dalton professed, watching Katherine shoot was pure joy. She had a talent and charm that made watching her pure fun. You couldn't help but cheer for her. She reminded him a little of the stories of Annie Oakley from years before. Though even Katherine would say she wasn't as crack of a shot as Annie.

"I can't say. I hope she does."

Scanning the list from a distance, Thad recognized all the names on the men's list and the two names on the women's list. He and Amos were the only men signed up for the elite contest. There were cash prizes for the men's and elite, but nothing for the women's. Women weren't supposed to compete, though Thad thought the lack of a prize for the women was purely greed on Mr. Slade's part.

"I wouldn't bother the banker with asking him about Kitty," Dalton said. "She annoys him and he'll say no. Especially with how her father isn't here. He probably hasn't made his bank payment in two months since he disappeared. So, Slade is not going to extend a hand to Kitty or any of her family."

If only there were another way, Thad wondered. But he'd been given the task of enriching the town and making it a better place for families to live with the proceeds that came from the annual shooting contest. Last year, he'd been able to purchase new much-needed desks for the school. The year before that, he'd been able to buy new hymnals for the two new churches in town.

Enrichment. Not charity. As much as he'd like to help the Horwaths and especially Katherine, his hands were firmly tied. "You're probably right," he said. "But you're also right in that we have to do something to help the Horwaths. They are part of this community and have lived right outside of town for longer than I can remember."

"Her pa came in 1889 when his wife was round with Kitty in her belly." Dalton laughed, wheezed, then spit a wad of chew across the room, hitting a brass spittoon behind the counter. "Kitty looks a lot like her mom did then. Like a willow tree with light hair." He laughed again.

The vision of Katherine in a light-green dress like the delicate willow branches near the river filled Thad's thoughts, and he headed for the door almost as fast as Katherine had. He couldn't help her, not when it came to the competition. No matter how much he wanted to.

2

Hannah Longfellow waved from her seat at the café where she and Kitty usually met for coffee when she was in town. Heat crawled up Kitty's cheeks. She wouldn't even be able to spend the penny it cost for a cup of hot water today.

The moment Kitty arrived at the table, Hannah helped her unwrap her scarf from around her neck, then took her hands and rubbed them. "Kitty, your hands are like ice. I'm forever forgetting my mittens everywhere, so Blake makes me leave a spare in the car. Take these, and I won't take no for an answer." Her dark-haired friend's eyes gleamed. "I've already ordered a carafe and two cups. Come, sit and talk."

Kitty took the seat across from Hannah and tossed her scarf and new mittens next to her. Pa and Ma would've scolded her for taking charity. She closed her eyes against the memory. It wasn't charity if a friend gave her a gift. Even if she couldn't repay it.

"Thank you. I didn't know you'd be in town today." Kitty waited until her hands quit shaking to pour a steaming cup of coffee for herself. The aroma wafting from Hannah's cup made her mouth water. It had been over a month since their own aluminum package of coffee beans had run through the percolator for the third and final time. When flour was a need, coffee was a luxury.

"Blake reminded me of the contest." Hannah smiled, showing a dimple. "I keep needling him about entering himself, but he says it's not good for a lawman to do that sort of thing. If he loses, people might take that as a cue to come to town and commit crime. I don't see the sense, but that's his reasoning."

Kitty glanced around the small shop. Women sat in dark but colorful walking attire, sipping coffee, and sharing conversation in loud bursts. Laughter bubbled from the back corner.

Hannah continued her chatter. "He's talking to the gunsmith and told me he'd be at least an hour. I'd hoped you would come into town. I didn't want to drive out to get you so I could have a visit. Your mother has been so…" Hannah scrunched her face. "I don't have a word for what I want to say, and I don't want to sound unkind or disrespectful."

That was better than most of the town. Ma had told people in no uncertain terms that she wouldn't listen to talk about Aspen Horwath. If they wanted to talk like fools, they could do so outside of her hearing.

"Distant?" Kitty tried to fill in Hannah's feeling,

then took her first sip of coffee. Too hot, she sucked in a breath against the sudden pain on her tongue.

"Partly. She doesn't want to hear from anyone. My last visit, she kept watching the window as if someone was going to see I was there." Hannah laid her hands crossed on the table. "I tried not to take it to heart."

"I'm glad you didn't. Ma and Pa didn't love each other—that much I know. But she's also lost without him. He may not have provided well for us, but he did provide." Kitty's fingers were now warm enough that color brightened them up to the last joint. They were gray from there to the tips.

"Ugh, don't look now. Nancy Powers just came in." Hannah ducked her head, hiding her face.

Kitty didn't need to look over her shoulder to hear Nancy's overly happy voice greeting everyone as she walked by before she stopped and lingered near the corner of Kitty's table.

"If it isn't Kitty Horwath. I just came into town to see who would be in the shooting contest, and I noticed your name wasn't on the list. Your daddy too poor to help you enter?" A fake pout slid down her face. "Or maybe you're too busy shooting rabbits to have time to shoot at targets." She bumped the table with her hip, splashing hot coffee over the lip of Kitty's cup and onto her thin dress. "Oh, I'm so sorry." Her fake apology dripped with sarcasm. Success gleamed in her eyes. "I'll send someone over to help clean up the mess," she said over her shoulder as she sashayed toward a table instead of alerting the server standing behind the counter.

Hannah stood and helped blot at the painfully hot liquid drenching Kitty's skirt. "That woman is vile. Stay away from her if you can."

People stared from across the room, curious about what had happened. Kitty shooed away Hannah's help and draped a napkin over her lap to hide the stain. The ride home would be cold, but her blood was heated enough from the exchange to keep her toasty.

"I didn't know you knew her," Kitty said.

Hannah replaced the sloshed coffee in Kitty's cup, then sighed. "That is a long story, and I think the way she acted is close to her true character from what I've seen. Fake in every way."

"Except her money, which is the one part that gives her the right." Kitty would never want to treat people like that, but she'd borne the brunt of it from others for years. People didn't seem to think she minded the abuse.

"Money is no excuse," Hannah said. "My family had money, and my pa would've slapped my face if I'd talked to anyone in that way or treated them like she did to you. With the exception of the Douglases, but that's a long story." She tilted her head slightly. "It is interesting that she stopped at our table though, and obviously seeing you bothered her. She didn't do anything to anyone else. I wonder what it is about you that bothers her so much?" Hannah sipped her coffee and glanced out the clean window.

Kitty bit her lip and ran her finger along the top of the mug, feeling the warmth seep through her. She wasn't sure why, but Nancy had mentioned the shooting competition, the one she had to figure out how to enter...as a man.

THAD'S WALKING cane clicked against the brick-lined street as he hurried his pace to the end of town. He'd hoped to catch up with Katherine, but she had to have dashed into some establishment and he didn't have the time to look for her. Especially when he had no legitimate reason to seek her.

Jack Danger pushed away from the shadowed wall of the tobacco shop and fell into step alongside him. "Morning."

Thad lifted his chin and smiled in silent greeting. Jack wanted to work for Thad. He'd asked on many occasions and his persistence was working, but Thad had no openings at the moment, especially for a boy of seventeen.

"Any work for me?" Jack shoved his hands into his pockets, fighting off the bitter chill in the air.

Thad slowed his steps. "I do, actually." He dug out his money clip and pulled out three paper dollars.

Jack whistled low. "What's that for?"

"I want you to take this money to the grocer. Get the best deal you can on some flour, sugar, coffee, and salt. Whatever is left is yours for your trouble."

The boy's mouth dropped open and he stopped, letting Thad get a few steps ahead until he ran to catch up. "Are you serious?"

"Yes. Then I want you to take those items out to the

Horwath place. Mrs. Horwath might not want to take them. The second part of your job is to sweet-talk her into letting you leave them with her."

"But, Thad... The Horwath pride is legendary. She won't take them. What am I supposed to do with them if she won't?"

Thad stopped, allowing him to look the boy in the eyes. The job was important, and Jack was just persistent and kind enough to get the job done. "I have faith in you," Thad said and tipped his hat as he left Jack to do the work he'd given.

Katherine wasn't the same as her parents. Thad had noticed that she accepted small gifts at church from the group who helped members in need, usually when her mother wasn't looking. Which gave him another idea. That few dollars of food wouldn't last long. Especially since the four other children in the Horwath home were growing boys.

He glanced toward the new, large church at the edge of town. He'd go visit the parson in the next few days and see what could be done for the Horwaths. If he went to the church where both of them attended, Katherine would be sure to find out and she might wonder why he was suddenly so interested in her and her family. He couldn't explain the fascination himself, except that it was there. Perhaps it was the Holy Spirit prodding him to do something with the blessings he'd received. Even as he had that thought, however, he brushed it away.

His thoughts turned to Katherine because she was

everything he desired in a woman but couldn't have. Men were forever wanting what they were told they should have no business with, and the woman that intrigued him topped that list. If only he were as interested in Nancy Powers as she seemed to be in setting up a match. Then he would have no room in his thoughts for Katherine Horwath.

The sun just peered over the top of the buildings along the street but didn't warm his skin. He had to hurry or the order of wood for the new skating rink wouldn't be ready in time for the shooting contest. Then again, if they didn't sell more tickets, he wouldn't be building one.

Reaching the bank, he resolutely headed inside. Dalton may have been right that Mr. Slade wouldn't listen to anything having to do with the Horwaths, but Thad owed it to Katherine to at least ask about a prize for the women. Especially if they didn't allow women to shoot against the men.

Mr. Slade sat at his desk in his large office with the door open. His secretary sat at a desk near the door, bent over a ledger, his slick hair shined to perfection. Thad made his way toward the secretary, then stopped in front of his desk. "I'd like a minute with Mr. Slade, if he's available."

Before the man could look up and answer, Mr. Slade waved him in. "Easton! Come on in. Sit." He pointed to the chair on the other side of his desk.

As a precaution, Thad closed the door behind him. He wouldn't want anyone to hear what he had do say and make assumptions about Katherine or their relationship. Honestly, if she had a father to come in and speak for her, he'd have no right to speak on her behalf, but everyone knew the man was missing.

"Katherine Horwath came to the pawnbroker to sign up for the contest today."

Mr. Slade nodded and pursed his lips. "I was beginning to think she was going to skip the competition altogether. That would be a slap in the face after what I did for her."

What he'd done was allow her to pay to compete, Thad thought. *How generous.* "You and I both know her family is in need. She should have the chance to win a prize just like every other competitor. We should add a prize in the women's competition or let the winner of both divisions shoot with the elite shooters."

Mr. Slade laughed outright. When Thad was sure he was about to stop, he started up again until he laughed so hard tears ran down his cheeks. He reached for his handkerchief. "You must be joking. We barely make enough money on this competition as it is, and you want me to give away *more* of the money?" His eyes narrowed. "I see no good reason to allow women to shoot against men. That's asking for trouble. If you let women shoot, you'll be the only one to compete against them. No one else will. All the competitors and onlookers will laugh you right out of town. I won't risk that."

Thad had feared as much. "Thanks for your time," he said and turned to leave. There was no point in arguing. Mr. Slade wouldn't change his mind, and he controlled the money for the competition. That meant Thad would have to help Katherine out in some other more creative way.

3

Kitty watched as Thad moved around inside the lumberyard office. He was easy to spot, even from a distance, with his height and bearing. He held himself well, like a wealthy person.

She flinched in the cold, her fingertips icy even in the new mittens. He was a prosperous man, and she needed to put aside her childish infatuation with him. What she had to do would put a wall between them that she would never be able to cross, even if her status as poor didn't already.

"What do you want me to do, Kitty?" Jack Danger shifted his weight back and forth, rubbing his hands together. "I've got a job to do, and I need to get to it."

"I'm sorry, Jack. I shouldn't have kept you waiting." She'd wanted to make sure Thad wasn't around near the pawnshop to ask questions when Jack signed her up under the elite shooters. Dalton wouldn't question a name he didn't know because Jack did odd jobs for everyone.

Thad would.

She tugged her mitten off and dug in her pocket for the few coins that had weighed against her leg all morning. That dollar was all that stood between her and poverty. She held her hand out above Jack's open palm and hesitated. Would the money be better used elsewhere? Ma desperately needed flour, and a dollar would buy quite a bit.

Jack shook his outstretched hand. "Come on, Kitty. It's cold out here."

She sighed, letting the coins drop. "You understand what you need to do?"

Jack nodded and pursed his lips. "I ain't daft. I'm to go into the pawnbroker and sign up Edwin Carlton for the elite competition. If Dalton asks me who he is, I'm to say that I don't know, that I was paid to sign him up."

Kitty gave a nod and shoved her hand back in the mitten, wishing she could give both of them to Jack. He looked plum frozen. "Go, warm up in the pawnshop."

"I'll get your chore done, then go do what I was paid to do this afternoon. I'll get warm when I know that I'll have a few coins for supper tonight." He dashed off down the street.

Two jobs in one day. Jack was moving up in the world.

Kitty turned and gave one final glance over to the lumberyard. Thad stood outside now, talking to a man she didn't recognize. Thad wore a tailored shirt and trousers that fit him perfectly. He'd rolled his sleeves up to help the man move some lumber to his wagon, his arms flexing with the strain.

Most wealthy men she knew didn't raise a finger. They paid other people to work for them. Thad was certainly one of a kind. She'd gone to him a month earlier and asked for a job at the yard. He'd flushed a light crimson at the idea and said he was sorry, but hiring a woman to do that job just wasn't done. He'd offered to take her in as a secretary, but that wouldn't do any good because she'd never been particularly good with books or numbers. Her aim and her strength were her best qualities far as she could tell.

Ma said she took after Pa, at least all the good parts. Kitty wasn't a swindler like her pa. They all knew he wasn't honest like he should be, so Ma had taught all her children to be better, to be God-fearing, which meant they had to be honest. Maybe Pa would still be alive if he'd been God-fearing like the rest of them.

Kitty tugged her coat tighter around her and wished it still had buttons to secure it closed against the wind. Those had long been pilfered to make other clothing. Nothing went to waste in the Horwath house, not even buttons. And certainly not opportunities.

God had given her a gift, and she had to use it to the best of her ability to provide for her family. If she didn't, her wily uncle would come and scoop up the chance to take all six of them on as free labor. If there were any other way to avoid becoming her uncle's unpaid servant, she hadn't thought of it.

"Are you ready to go home?"

Her brother Alex's voice made her jump. "You nearly scared me out of my skin."

"That's not something I ever want to see." He chuckled. "I worked for an hour this morning to pay for our spot at the livery, but our time is almost up. We've got to go. You got done what you needed to?" He puffed warm breath onto the heels of his hands.

"I did." Her stomach clenched at the idea of tricking Thad. He'd be so disappointed in her, and the idea of seeing hurt or disappointment on his face almost made her want to run over and tell Dalton the truth. Almost.

"Good. You'll win that prize, and then we can send money to Uncle Damion for the rent." He slowly headed toward the livery.

Kitty fell into step alongside him. "He hasn't come yet. Maybe he won't." Though there was little hope of that. Both her pa and his brother milked situations for all they were worth. Her uncle would see assigning them work without pay as repayment for food, lodging, and for the house payments Pa had missed. He was loathsome, and Ma wasn't safe if he came around now that Pa was gone.

Kitty sighed with resolution. "He'll come. When Pa doesn't come for their usual spring meeting to discuss the loan he took from Uncle Damion, he'll come to collect."

Alex ducked his head. "If we had the money to pay

him back, we'd be fine. He'd leave us be. But he'll see that repayment as an open door to do what he wants. Pa never should've borrowed money from a scoundrel."

"It's not like the bank would've given him any money to buy another home." And it wasn't like he'd done anything good with the house anyway. Pa never did. They'd stayed poor because Pa could never see beyond the day in front of him. He spent resources to fill an immediate need, even spending more than he should because he felt it was an emergency.

"True. I guess we'll just wait," said Alex. "Pa would've gone in ten days. That leaves us about two weeks before Uncle Damion comes to see what's the matter."

Alex opened the door to the barn and held it for Kitty to go through. The boys had all learned manners from Ma. In fact, if it hadn't been for Ma, they'd all be complete outcasts in Deadwood. Kitty owed Ma everything, even if that meant working for Uncle Damion to pay off Pa's debt and keeping her uncle far away from Ma.

Alex led the horse out the back to where the wagon waited, and Kitty followed, helping where she could.

"Kitty, wait!"

Jack ran toward her. She glanced quickly at Alex and hoped Jack didn't say anything about the job she'd had him do, especially since she hadn't been able to pay Jack for the job and because her brother would scold her—both for lying about who she was and for asking Jack to help without giving him something in return.

"Jack, what is it?"

"You'll need to stop by the market. There's an order waiting for you. A good one."

Alex glanced at her, his brows dipping. "I didn't order anything," he said.

"I didn't, either." She had no money to do anything like that. And Pa didn't have a line of credit because they couldn't pay it back. She looked at Jack. "Are you sure?"

"Yes. I was asked to run and catch up to you. I didn't have time to go see Dalton yet. I got waylaid by the grocer." Jack laughed.

Alex stared at her without uttering a word, his look at her alone asking why Jack would say that.

"Thank you. I'll go see what the fuss is about." Kitty turned back to Alex, letting Jack continue on his way, hopefully going to see Dalton.

"So… We need to stop by the grocer. But why would Jack need to say he hadn't visited Dalton yet? Seems odd, since that's where the signup is." Alex affixed the last harness clip and waited for her to answer.

The boy—fast turning to a man—was far too observant for his own good. "I have no idea. I think he was making conversation."

Alex threw his head back and laughed. "You are the worst liar, Kitty. Honesty runs through your veins. I guess I'll just have to trust you. What do you think is going on with the grocer? I know we didn't have any credit. If we did, Ma would've bought food a month ago."

Kitty licked her cold lips, but regretted the action immediately as she felt the biting wind burn her tender skin. "I'm sure I don't know. Let's go see and get home. A warm fire will be good."

Alex climbed up into the seat, and she followed on her side. As they approached the grocer, a stack of packages sat on the boardwalk out in front and a boy stood next to it, guarding them.

"Miss Kitty! I'm glad you didn't take any longer," the boy called to her. "Cecil told me I had to stand here and make sure you, and no one else, got this. He said I needed to wave you down if you tried to ride out of town without getting your food."

Having the packages outside was even more odd, Kitty thought. Why wouldn't Cecil want her to come into the store to get them? "Who bought all of this? Because I surely didn't."

The boy shrugged a thin shoulder. "Not sure. You going to take it? I want to go back inside. I'm needed to stock the shelves, and I can leave as soon as I'm finished."

Kitty shooed the boy off, but sat still as Alex climbed down to load the wagon. Maybe Hannah had purchased a few things for them? She'd known Kitty was in such a state that she couldn't afford her own coffee. That had to be it. She'd write a note of thanks to Hannah later and say a prayer that Ma had a stamp laying around for her to use.

"What's Ma going to say about this?" Alex climbed

in and grabbed hold of the lines. "It sure looks like charity, and you know what she says about that."

Kitty braced herself on the seat. "Hopefully Ma sees the need and doesn't ask any questions." Just like her own situation with the shooting contest.

4

Ma had promised she wouldn't touch that coffee from the mercantile. She'd been calling it "devil's brew" for the last two days, but she sure eyed it with longing that morning. Kitty had been trying to ply Ma with truth, that a gift wasn't a bad thing. It was generosity, and God called on people to be generous to those who had less.

So far, Ma wasn't buying it though.

Alex and Kitty's other three brothers had made meals with the food straight away, and Ma was too hungry to say no to that. But the coffee, that wasn't food and she hadn't touched it. Yet.

"What's that Thad Easton doing coming this way? He must be lost." Ma laughed. "I don't think I've ever seen him come out here before."

"Thad?" Kitty's voice was a little more of a shriek than she intended. Had he figured out who the mystery name on the signup sheet was? If he did, he'd be so disappointed with her.

"Yes, Thad. Clean out your ears, girl." Ma slapped the table. "Better put on more of that stuff from the store. Can't have no highfalutin' city folk sit at our table without something to offer. And go find Alex. I can't imagine he'd be out here to see anyone else."

Kitty held in an offended sniffle. "Yes, ma'am." But she'd take her time with the coffee so Thad would arrive to the door before she went to find Alex. If she weren't in the house when he arrived, Ma might never tell her why he'd come.

As Thad strode with purposeful steps toward the house, Kitty noticed a small wooden box tucked under his arm. All the heat drained from her body. That looked like the case the pink pistol was in. Why did he have it with him?

She sloshed water over the burner and sizzling steam erupted all around her. "Ma, you'll have to get the door." She reached for a kitchen towel and waved away the steam, hoping her mistake didn't damage the top of the stove. Ma would scold her good if she ruined something they couldn't fix or replace.

"Everything all right in here?" Thad's deep voice came from the doorway.

Heat crept up Kitty's cheeks. "I just spilled a little water over the hot stove. Just call me clumsy." She giggled to cover her embarrassment.

"I wouldn't dream of it." He appeared out of the mist. "Anything I can do to help?"

Why did he have to be so kind to her? Why

couldn't he be suspicious and overbearing, like all the other men she knew? Then her chest wouldn't flutter like a butterfly every time he was near her.

He moved back slightly, giving her room to breathe, and set the wooden box on the table. Ma shuffled over to the stove. "Gracious, me. What did you do?"

"I spilled. Nothing too terrible." Though now the room smelled like scalded coffee and a white stain covered the top of the woodstove.

Ma looked at Thad. "Did you come to see Alex? I can send Kitty out to fetch him." Ma scowled at Kitty like she wasn't fit to boil water.

"Actually, I came to speak to Katherine. If I may?" He glanced at Kitty and gave her a reassuring smile.

"Me?" Kitty asked, surprised. He'd held the door open for her two days before, but that was as close as they'd ever come to having a conversation that had nothing to do with either his business or the weather.

"Yes. If I may?" He waited.

"Well, go sit on the porch with him, girl," Ma said. "Don't keep him in the smoky kitchen."

Kitty's face heated like she'd set her cheek down on the stove. Ma made it sound like Thad was courting her, which was exactly why Pa had put that bench out in front of the house. Pa had even teased her, calling it a sparking bench. For the briefest moment, Kitty allowed herself to think what *sparking* with Thad Easton would be like, but since she'd never so much as bussed Ma on the cheek, much less put her lips to a man's, the daydream didn't get far.

She wiped her clammy hands and followed Thad as he gathered the box and headed back outside. At least the weather was warmer that day than it had been two days before when she'd seen him. The hills were like that—fickle. Warm one day, chill you to the bone the next.

Thad sat down on the bench as if he had not a clue or care what the bench was meant for. Maybe he didn't. Kitty settled next to him and gripped her legs just above the knees, only then noticing how shabby her skirt was next to his fine clothing.

"What can I do for you, Mr. Easton?" Although she'd thought of him as Thad for so long when she'd dreamed about him rescuing her from her poverty, remembering to use the proper name had become difficult. But all those dreams were made of childish things. Real life wasn't like the tales of old. There was no mystery or romance in the real world. Just hunger and survival.

"I saw you eyeing this in the pawnshop the other day. I know you don't usually accept gifts, but I couldn't imagine this fitting quite as nicely in any other hand but yours." He opened the box and turned it for her to see.

Her heart caught in her throat, and she couldn't speak. The pistol was even more beautiful now than it had been in the store. She reached out and touched the cold metal of the barrel. It had been well taken care of by whomever had owned it. "I wonder where it came from?"

Thad chuckled. "I'm not sure. I didn't inspect it. I

just remembered Dalton saying that the owner had until this morning to pick it up. His loss. It's a lovely piece. But do you think you can shoot it?" He dug in the large front pocket of his long coat and pulled out a small bag with string tying the top. "I bought a few rounds so you could try."

"Shoot it? Now?" Kitty asked. In front of Thad? She swallowed, knowing she was being rude. He'd given her this incredible gift, and she hadn't even thanked him yet. "I mean…of course. Thank you." She stood and headed for the back of the house where she and her brothers would set up cans on the fence on the rare occasion Ma bought anything canned.

As soon as they arrived there, Thad said, "There, now let's see how she shoots. The gun, of course. I already know your capability."

Kitty opened the cylinder with a flick. She wasn't sure how she was ever going to repay Thad for his generosity, but she'd start by giving him the best target show he'd ever seen.

THE PEARL HANDLE of the pistol shimmered in the weak morning sunlight as Thad braced himself behind Katherine, out of her way. He'd been shooting since he was about five, and it was obvious by how she handled the little revolver that she'd had just as much, if not more, experience.

As she methodically loaded the pistol, he noted how the gun fit her hand quite well, even though she was small for a woman her age. Most men he knew would've showboated, given this opportunity. They'd have made a great production of loading the pistol, taking aim, and making great commentary about each target as they hit it. *If* they hit it.

But Katherine didn't look back at him, didn't look for his approval. She innately seemed to understand that he knew what she was about to do, and didn't offer him any warning or direction. With no fanfare whatsoever, she pulled up the pistol in a fluid motion to the level of her hip and took out each target, one second after the next in perfect time. Her shooting was like music to his ears.

He wanted to shout, "Bravo!" and clap, but the look on her face said any reaction would be too much. Instead he settled for, "Well done. I do believe that the pistol is accurate."

She gave a slight nod. "It's slightly high and to the right, but I can get used to that. No sense in having a gunsmith look at it." She gently laid the pistol down on the table next to the wooden case.

Her pensive brow worried him. Why wouldn't she say anything? Had he offended her with the gift? He'd known Katherine's ma hated favors, but he'd thought Katherine would accept it. "Have I offended you? I didn't mean to. I noticed you seemed to take an interest in it. I was worried you wouldn't get the chance to have it, what with…" He bit back the rest of what he'd planned to say. Talking to her made him forget he couldn't be completely forthright as he was with any other man.

She wasn't any other man. She was a woman and had feelings.

"I don't know how to pay you back for this. I can't, truth be told. It's a beautiful gun, but it shouldn't belong to me. Maybe you should give it to Nancy. *She could repay you.*" She swallowed loudly enough for him to hear.

"If Miss Powers wanted the pistol, she had the means to go buy it herself. If you feel like you need to repay me for the pistol, then come help me over the next four days as I set up for the shooting event. But do not feel like repayment is necessary. It's not. I merely wanted to give you a gift." Perhaps too nice of a gift for someone he wasn't supposed to know or have anything to do with, but the deed was done.

"Help you? In town? Every day?" Kitty's chin raised and she met his gaze. "You want my help?"

"I do. I would like that. The students from the school are helping after their daily studies, but most of them know nothing about shooting. You couldn't help set up any course where you're going to participate, but that shouldn't be difficult since you haven't signed up at all."

She slowly shook her head. "I shouldn't."

"Is it because you're going to register to shoot? I hope you'll consider signing up. Without you, no one in Deadwood will watch the women's competition, and then Mr. Slade will consider removing it. Just because your family is going through a brief hardship doesn't mean future women shootists should suffer. I could pay you the dollar for your work so you could sign up."

Katherine picked up the pistol and looked at it like it was the most precious thing she owned. "You're right, of course. I can help setting up the measurements, but not the targets. And you've given enough. I'll find my own dollar."

Thad told himself that his heart picked up its clattering because he would have the help he needed, but he suspected it was actually because for the next few days he'd have a perfectly legitimate excuse to talk to Katherine Horwath, and none of the Deadwood busybodies could say anything about it.

5

The smart wooden case for the pistol rested on the kitchen table, and Ma ran her finger along the edge of it as she sipped her morning coffee. She'd finally relented that morning and allowed herself one mug, but not a sip more.

"And Thad got this for you? But he didn't want to come in and talk to me? Maybe he's not as respectable as I thought. Just because your pa isn't here doesn't mean I'll just let you go off with any man who brings over a gift. Fine or not."

Kitty swallowed hard. "It's not like that. He simply wanted to do something for me."

"Now girl, I don't put any credence in luck or anything of the sort, but did you look inside this case? I don't think Thad only had a gift in mind."

"Inside? It's just a pistol. The case is beautiful, but..."

Ma pulled out a narrow sheet of paper. With shaky

fingers, she laid it out on the table, then slid it toward Kitty. The sheet had yellowed a little but was still easy to read. Kitty hadn't noticed any paper in there when she'd looked at the pistol the day before. "Where did you find this?"

"It was tucked in the top, just visible if you'd care to look. Though I suppose you were too busy looking at the gun, and the giver, to take any notice."

The giver… "Oh, no." The note—she read it over. This couldn't be happening. No. No note was going to tell her she had to fall in love or, worse, that Thad would be saddled with her the rest of his life. She folded the paper back up and carefully returned it where Ma had found it. "I'll just give it back to him. He can give the gun to someone more suitable."

Ma stood from her seat so fast Kitty jumped back. Ma thrust her fists to her hips so hard she *harumphed* softly from the force. "Just who do you think is more suitable than you? Nancy Powers? That girl thinks the world of herself. She doesn't need a man to tell her she's wonderful because she already believes as much. You're just as suitable as anyone else."

"You know that's not true, Ma. You know that I can't be the kind of woman to catch Thad's attention." No matter how much she wished she could be. She was poor and he was not. If he ever were interested in her, they'd have to leave Deadwood, which would hurt Thad. He'd have to start over from the very beginning somewhere else. Women like her just didn't marry men like him.

Ma slowly sat back down. "I wish I could make

things different for you. I can't say that I haven't prayed, time and again, for the Lord to lift us out of this place. I know now I never should've married your father. He wasn't my first choice, but he treated me well. That's all in the past though. I don't want you making the same mistakes I did. I only have one daughter to give all the wisdom I've learned over the years, and that starts with not settling for the first person to give you something nice. Aim for a man with a good heart."

Kitty had never understood why Ma was so opposed to gifts, but she wondered if Pa didn't have a big part in that now. Asking now seemed like too little, too late. "But Thad did give me a nice gift."

"More than that, he gave you a chance. He came out here. Walked out here, instead of riding in some carriage to show off his wealth, and gave a gift that mattered to you. Do you think any of those debutantes in town would appreciate a pistol as a gift? Their fathers might, but they wouldn't."

Kitty hadn't thought about that. Even Nancy, who could shoot, wouldn't want a gun as a gift. "But he's still wealthy, and I'm not. I can't even afford coffee or anything. We're a week away from losing everything to Uncle Damion."

Ma flinched. "Let's not talk about him right now. You said you need to go into town to help Mr. Easton set up the contest. Do that. Be the best helper he could ask for. And…" Ma laid a weathered hand over the pretty wooden box. "Don't discount what the letter says just because you think it doesn't fit you. David didn't look the part of a king, but he was. That didn't mean he wasn't destined for greatness."

"I'm no David." But she wouldn't lie to God and say she didn't wish she were someone Thad could look on with favor.

Ma turned Kitty around and tugged a hairbrush from her front apron pocket. With gentle strokes, Ma brushed through her daughter's wavy hair and tugged it up into respectable submission. "There. I can't provide you with a perfect dress or shoes, but I can make your hair look pretty, and the face God gave you is lovely. Let your attitude do the rest."

Kitty was knowledgeable about shooting, and Thad had said that's why he needed her help. Maybe if she helped him as best she could, he would see her as more than charity. Maybe Ma—and by extension from the note, Annie Oakley—was right.

JACK STOOD next to Thad at the lumberyard, shifting from one foot to the other. He did that when he was nervous, making Thad wonder what the boy was up to.

"You see, it's just that..." Jack glanced over to the huge pile of 4 x 4 wood rails stacked a few feet away. "I don't think I can do the job. I'm just not cut out for it."

"Like haggling with the grocer?" Thad intentionally raised his brow as he looked at the boy. He knew it made him look more aristocratic than he felt, but he needed to know that both Katherine's family and Jack had been taken care of. He hadn't stayed inside the Horwath home long enough to know for sure, though he'd witnessed coffee on the stove.

"I did as you asked! I went in there straight away while Kitty was in the café with her friend. She didn't stay there long and I wanted to find out if she was leaving town, so I went to talk to her. She had a job for me to do, too." Jack smacked his hand over his mouth.

"What job was that?" Katherine had no money to pay Jack, and the boy didn't work for free, that much Thad knew.

"Can't say. But I did what you asked me to do. You can get a list from Cecil. I was in too much of a hurry to get one that day." Jack crossed his arms and glared up at Thad. "You got anything else for me to do besides dig post holes?"

"The correct way to ask is 'do you have anything else for me to do?' and the answer is yes. But I'll need this work done either way. Hitch up the lumberyard horse to the pull cart and move those posts to the top of the hill on the opposite end of town as Moriah Cemetery."

"The flat land. But that's a mile outside of town. Will people walk?"

"They always have in the past." It was the only area where they could safely set up targets, unless they wanted to have a shootout right up the main street. Which didn't seem the best idea for an event meant to help the town prosper.

"That will take some time." Jack frowned. "I don't

know how I can move those poles all by myself onto the cart. How much do they weigh?"

Thad had no idea and no time to argue over it. Katherine should be coming into town any minute, and he wanted to devote his attention to her as soon as she arrived. "If it's an issue, you can share your pay with someone else and have help. You could hire someone. It's a worthy thing to do."

Jack's jaw dropped slack. "Hire someone else? Me? I'd never thought that was possible." He turned and wandered back toward the tall stack of lumber put there by Thad's men to build targets for the event.

Just then Katherine appeared at the end of the street with a basket over her arm. Thad had hoped she wouldn't bring a lunch so he could treat her to something from the café, but he knew she wouldn't expect that from him. Katherine never expected anything from anyone.

The moment she caught his eye, he couldn't help but smile back at her. She moved so carefully up the street toward him, how he'd managed to see her amidst all the others in the street he didn't know. Thinking on that would only make him worry.

She came to stand beside him. "I'm afraid I wasn't sure what to wear, so I chose work clothes."

Thad noted her leather gloves and apron. How had he missed those as she'd been walking? Right…he'd been distracted by her lovely face. "Today I want to draw out a plan. Jack is going to deliver the supplies outside of town to the site, but before we can start setting anything up, we need to draw out exactly what will go where."

She nodded and glanced toward the pawnshop. "I didn't have a chance to go sign up."

"We still have time." He hadn't planned to charge her anything for the pistol, so if she needed his help, he'd also pay for her entry.

Katherine pursed her lips, then let them relax. "Thank you. About the pistol… There was a note inside. I know you'll think this is silly, but I don't think you meant to give that gun to me."

Thad took a step back, trying to understand what she could mean. The gun was practically made for her. Why would she think anyone else should have it? "I intended to buy it for you. It's yours. Enjoy it. Also"—he glanced up and down the street, hoping for a moment of privacy—"Mr. Slade won't change his mind about offering a prize for the women's division. But I don't think that's right. I have the means to fix it, and I am. There is now a five-dollar prize for winning the women's competition."

"Five dollars? That's almost a week's worth of Pa's pay. When he worked." She glanced away, and pink climbed up her cheeks.

"I know it's not much in comparison, but it's what I can do without making Mr. Slade angry enough to take me off the board."

She slowly shook her head and attempted a smile. "It's very generous. But don't you think it's bad for me to be helping you if I'm planning to participate?"

"Not at all!" He'd hoped she would ask that. "I've

always struggled to find help in creating the elite range. Since I am the one who has to make it, everyone assumes I have an advantage. With you here, that advantage is gone. I'm sure you'll understand how your help is really making things easier for me, too."

Thad had expected her to respond with excitement —at the very least to see his idea as a good one—but she merely firmed her jaw and nodded toward the lumberyard. "Should we go get started?" she asked.

While his office would ensure fewer people would see him talking to Katherine, he wanted her to be comfortable, which meant his tiny office was out of the question. "Let's share a coffee at the café. My treat."

Her eyes watered slightly, but she didn't disagree as she let him lead the way.

6

Kitty arrived in town the following day and headed straight for the site where they would be placing the targets. Thad had told her to meet him there since he'd started as soon as the sun had come up.

Schoolchildren raced up the hill of the site, their teacher, Mrs. Bain, following behind. Kitty held in a groan. Beside Mrs. Bain was Nancy Powers, chatting animatedly with a pistol strapped to her shapely hip. Kitty knew she wasn't there to work or to help with the children, but she'd say she was. All the while, Kitty would look like a ragamuffin next to her, especially since she'd worn a pair of Alex's trousers so she could move around more easily.

Thad stood next to Jack at some distance, pointing from a large stack of lumber to various areas over the wide grassy field. Bright-green grass had shot up with the warmth of the day, and the land had gone from a dull brown to vibrant within hours. Kitty breathed deeply, relishing the scent of spring.

Thad noticed the children first, and one of the young girls ran right up to him. He bent slightly, picked her up and lifted her high, released her into the air, then caught her and set her back on her feet as the girl squealed in delight.

"Wipe your mouth, you're salivating over him. Not that he wouldn't make a fine father. And fine children for that matter." Nancy's acidic tone broke into Kitty's thoughts, and Leta laughed at her ribald comment.

"Am not." Though Kitty wiped her mouth with the back of her hand just in case. Thad cut a fine figure. Why wouldn't he catch her eye? His arms were corded from years of working with heavy lumber. Even now, as the owner, he still worked hard.

"You don't seriously think he'd ever look at you?" Nancy laughed and the teacher giggled next to her. "Look at you, in trousers. Your hair is a fright. Workman's gloves on your hands. *If* he sees you at all, he sees you as just another set of hands to do the work. He doesn't see you as a woman. I was asked by Mr. Easton to come and help keep an eye on the children while they help him. Why are you here?"

If Kitty said Thad had also asked her to help him, she would prove Nancy right—that she was nothing more than a pair of hands. And maybe she was. The little note inside the pistol case mocked her. Thad had given her the pistol, but he didn't know the note had been there any more than she had until it was too late.

That meant the prediction wouldn't work. If things like that ever did.

"I heard Thad offered a prize for winning the women's competition," Leta said, angling her head to look Kitty in the eyes.

"I'd heard that," Kitty said. She was thankful neither woman had waited to hear why she was there, though her clothing made the answer obvious anyway.

Nancy laughed. "When I win, I'll refuse the money and tell him he owes me a meal at the café instead. That will get everyone talking."

"You mean like he took Kitty to the café yesterday?" Leta blinked innocently.

Kitty clenched her teeth. So, Leta was there to be a gossip as much as help. She'd thought she was a friend of Nancy's.

"He took *you* to the café? Why would he do that? I can't believe he'd allow himself to be seen with you." Nancy stomped in the soft grass as she walked off in her fashionable boots.

"Good morning, ladies." Thad nodded their way, stopping Nancy. "I've sent the younger children down that way for you both to watch. I don't think they'd be much help, and I don't want them getting hurt. Katherine and I can manage the older ones with Jack."

Nancy sniffled softly. "I thought you'd be willing to take a look at my gun? It's quite nice and new, but I think I need help sighting it." Her voice took on an unnatural whine.

Thad glanced around him. "I'm afraid I don't have

time to do that if I'm going to get the contest set up. Why don't you ask the gunsmith? He'd be the one to help you move the sights." He turned away.

"Is that all you needed us to do? Just watch the little ones out in the sun all day?" Nancy seemed impatient and her lips pinched.

He glanced over his shoulder but stopped. "Yes. If it will be too hot for both of you, you can take them back down to the shade of the school."

Leta giggled behind her hand. "I'm all for heading back. We can have reading time."

"No. If Thad asked me to stay around, I'll stay around." Nancy marched after him instead of going with the children.

"I'd wondered how long she would actually help. Tell Thad I'm taking the children back near the school." Leta waved and walked away, leaving Kitty to wonder what she should do now.

Clearly Nancy was the better choice for a man like Thad. She was well-to-do and had beauty with many dresses, hats, and fancy things. Thad wouldn't need to buy anything for her, nor would the town mock him for taking Nancy as a bride.

Kitty trudged toward where the small group was waiting while Thad handed out directions. "Ah, there you are. I was worried you'd changed your mind." Thad smiled at her.

Nancy slid in close to him. "Whatever you need me to do, I can. Just tell me." She fluttered her lashes at him.

Thad stepped away from her and touched his chin.

"I'm not sure what I could have you do. Are you familiar with hammering or hauling?"

She bit her lip and looked up at him. "Well, no. But I can measure. I'm quite good at that. Don't you have to measure the distance of each target?"

He eyed Kitty for a moment before answering, "Yes, that does need to be done."

"Fine. I'll measure, and you can come along with me and pound in a marker at each spot. Then Kitty and Jack can follow behind us and dig the holes for the posts."

This wasn't what Kitty had agreed to, but Thad had given her a pistol and her discomfort would be temporary. She watched him hesitate, then give in.

"Sure. Let's get started."

ALL THAD HAD WANTED to do was spend a few days with Katherine, talking and working. He'd hoped to get to know her better. He'd hoped the town would see her value when he showed them she had value. But he couldn't work with Katherine if Nancy was plastered to his side. The two were like oil and water.

Nancy touched his bare arm with chilly fingers. "Goodness, you must work hard."

He shrugged, effectively moving her hand without being outwardly rude to her. "I've worked my entire life. I don't see that changing."

"You're so different from the other men in town.

They are either dirt poor or have aplenty and work in making money, not labor."

He hated to correct her, but Deadwood wasn't the land of the wealthy. "There are a small handful of men in this town who have made their fortunes without toiling. But most have worked hard. I point to the newspaper man, the hotelier, the chief at the fire department…" They'd all gone from nothing to making something of themselves. Unfortunately for him, they'd also all married well and would look down on him for taking a bride they considered inferior if he married Katherine. Why work so hard for what he had and then potentially lose it all for a needy family?

"You're so wise." Nancy stopped walking and drew out the string measure he'd brought with him that morning. "Where would you like the first set to be?"

Thad had thought about making this a real competition, like the ones he'd watched in Dodge City when he was younger, but Deadwood had always done things Wild West style. Just like the old shows with Wild Bill and Annie Oakley. They'd been limited by the area where people could see what the shooters were doing, as was the case now here in Deadwood. Thad had to make sure people could see, or they wouldn't come to future events.

"We'll set up ten ranges, each at longer distances, each twenty yards apart." He'd already discussed this with Katherine, and if she were working alongside him, he wouldn't have to explain.

"And where is the starting line? I'm assuming all the shooters will take aim from the same line, then the targets will all extend from there?"

Thad glanced over to where Katherine and Jack were moving the huge rig full of wooden posts out to the range. Those posts would hold the targets. "We'll start here. I wanted to give enough room for people to stand behind the shooters. In front of them obviously isn't safe, and even to the side is risky."

Nancy laughed. "That won't matter. We'll still have people pressing in closer than they should. Perhaps you should pound in one of your stakes here, and we can measure out the front line, then each range."

She was taking over, but her plan wasn't bad, so Thad said nothing. Instead, he grabbed the stake and gave it a few good whacks into the soft soil. As he looked back up at Nancy, he couldn't help but notice the gleam in her eye. This was going to be a very long day.

He finished measuring the line where shooters would aim as a few of the men he'd been thinking about arrived to help. They'd all donated toward the cost of the targets and the supplies for the roller rink, and the community donations provided the balance they needed to get the job done.

Thad tipped his hat to the men. "Good morning."

Mr. Slade rolled up his sleeves and glanced at Nancy. "I didn't expect to see you out here."

"I'm helping Thad." She inched her chin higher.

Mr. Slade turned and glanced over the whole area,

focusing on Jack and Katherine. "What are they doing? Can they be trusted? Kitty will most likely be shooting in the contest, and her father is less than trustworthy. Jack is little more than a skunk in a boy's coat."

"I have to agree with you. I don't think Thad should trust either of them." Nancy narrowed her eyes as she stared toward Katherine.

Just then, Katherine stood up straight and wiped her brow with the back of her arm. She was working with a hand drill, augering a hole for a post that would mark the start line. Jack stood next to her with a shovel, moving the dirt out of her way as she bent back down and slowly twisted the auger back out of the ground. The job was hard work, especially in the rocky soil around Deadwood.

"I need all the help I can get, and I trust both of them," Thad said.

"You trust them as long as they are over there digging holes." Mr. Slade laughed. "Best lock up your wallets, boys." He fished out his thick money clip from his pocket and held out his hand for everyone else's. "I'll walk them back to the bank for safekeeping."

Thad wanted to defend Katherine. She'd never done anything to deserve their anger or distrust beyond being Aspen's daughter, which would label her as a cheat and a thief her entire life. If she were never given the chance to change their minds, they never would.

"Oh, Mr. Slade?" Nancy waved to him as he was

leaving. "Can you take this with you? I'm worried Kitty will see my new pistol and want it for herself."

Mr. Slade took the small gun from her hands and looked it over. "My, that's a fine pistol. I'll put that away for you. It's good you're taking care of such a fine weapon."

Thad turned away so no one would see his frustration. If he continued to push these people to give Katherine a chance, would they turn on him? Would he lose his business in Deadwood, and was he willing to do that for her?

7

Sweat made Kitty's shirtwaist cling to her arms. At least she still had her chemise to protect her only good corset from all that dampness. Washing her chemise wasn't enjoyable, though she was sure it had soaked through.

"Katherine, I'm not sure what I would've done today without you." Thad appeared at her side, rolling down his sleeves.

Kitty hadn't missed that he'd waited to come talk to her until the only other person left in the area was Jack. All the men who made Deadwood as respectable as it was had left a few minutes before, though they'd seemed to linger as if warning him not to stay.

She peeled off her gloves but hid her hands, knowing there would be blisters from turning the auger all day. Jack had taken turns with her, but the boy was seventeen and not nearly strong enough to do all of it.

"I don't think you even stopped for lunch," Thad continued.

He'd noticed? She narrowed her eyes at him, wondering what he was trying to say. She hadn't been able to afford lunch at the café like everyone else, besides Jack, and Ma had been too tired to bake a loaf of bread the night before. Kitty hadn't realized that in time, so she hadn't had anything to bring in a lunch pail.

"I forgot my lunch at home." A lie, but only partially. She would've brought something had the bread been made.

"You must be starving. Can I get something for you on your way home?"

She did have to walk through town to go to her house, but after seeing Nancy flutter around Thad all day, she didn't have the heart to spend time with him now. Covered in dirt and sweat, she was no comparison to Nancy. "Thank you for offering, but I should get home to check on Ma. She's been home with Alex all day."

Her two younger brothers had been with the schoolboys, but they'd avoided her. She hadn't pressed them when they'd run off. She was in trousers, and schoolchildren could be particular. She didn't want them to be teased because of her.

Thad frowned slightly and motioned her over to a large basin sitting by the new firing tables one of the men had built. "I had one of the children go to town and draw water for everyone to wash their hands or splash their faces. It's out in the open so it will catch the rain, if we get any before the contest."

Kitty wanted to dunk her entire body in the cold water, but that wouldn't do. Instead, she dipped her hands in and splashed some of the water over her heated face. She'd had a hat, but her cheeks burned with heat that wouldn't go away.

Thad slowly swiped the water from her cheek and stared into her eyes. She swallowed hard. Nancy had claimed he didn't see Kitty as a woman and probably didn't see her at all, but his smoldering eyes said he very much saw her.

"Why don't I walk with you? I'd hoped to talk with you today and had no time," he said.

She stepped back, regaining her mind. "What did you need to talk to me about?" Maybe he had read the note and now he wanted the pistol back. He could give it to Nancy and that little rhyme would be fulfilled, just like so many before her. The list of people who'd been helped was fairly long on that sheet, honestly.

"Does the pistol shoot well?" Thad reached around her, guiding her toward town.

She hadn't wanted to leave Jack, but at some point he'd disappeared, leaving her alone with Thad on the hill. No one would think anything of it, though, because Thad would never do anything with her. The realization that they could be alone together and neither of their reputations would suffer froze her heart. The town knew better.

"The pistol shoots beautifully," she replied. But

was that really what he wanted to know about? She couldn't stop him if he wanted to walk alongside her, but hadn't he had his fill of people? He'd answered questions all day long with Nancy at his side.

"I'm glad. Then it was worth it."

She had to know if he'd seen the note. If he had, then perhaps he was toying with her. Perhaps he thought being kind to her in secret would be fun until she gave him her trust, then he could do something cruel in front of everyone. As it was, though Thad didn't seem the type, Mr. Slade had made it a point to tell her—loudly—that he was removing all temptation for either her or Jack to take anyone's money. It would be locked up in the bank.

"Did you know Annie Oakley once owned that pistol?" Kitty bit her lip, feeling the sunburn there the worst.

"Really? If that's the case, I'm surprised the price wasn't more." Thad eased his pace to match hers as they descended the steep hill down into Deadwood.

"You didn't know?" She had to be completely certain. If he hadn't known about the note, then he wasn't toying with her.

"No. If Dalton had been aware, I'm sure he would've charged me much more than he did. He charged a fair price for the quality of the item, but no more."

Thad's arm brushed against hers as they walked—an arm that had caught her attention more than once throughout the day. Her father had not been strong in the same way. She'd feared him, but not for his physical prowess. He was just good at making her frightened. He'd often told her he was sorry for teaching her to shoot so well because there were times she needed the smart beat out of her and he was afraid she'd shoot him if he tried.

Lord help her, she might have. So why didn't this man, much taller and stronger than her father, scare her when her father had?

FOLLOWING women home when they clearly didn't need his assistance wasn't Thad's way, but the entire day had left him frustrated and needing a few more minutes with Katherine. Unfortunately, the closer they came to her home, the more she seemed to be trying to shake him off her trail.

"I'm sure after such a long day, you've got work to do. You don't have to follow me all the way out to my place. It's a long walk back for you," Katherine said, glancing over her shoulder toward the bank.

Was she worried someone might see them talking together? "I don't mind. If you're tired, I can hitch a cart for us. It won't take but a minute."

She shook her head quickly. "No, no trouble. I don't want you to go out of your way for me. Oh, there's Nancy coming out of the bank…and heading this way."

He could hear the barely hidden groan in her voice. He would have mimicked it if he could. "You don't get along with her, do you?"

Katherine flinched and glanced at her shoes. He saw her wiggle her big toe through the thin leather. "Is it that obvious? That means I'm not being very Christian to her if you can see it. But she's none too kind to me, either."

He'd gotten the impression Nancy was more than a little jealous of Katherine, though he'd wager she would never admit as much. The mere idea that Katherine would have something Nancy wanted would be preposterous to her.

"If she treats you poorly, then I won't ask her to return to the work site. Then we can have peace while we finish up." He'd hoped to make her smile, but instead her eyes turned glassy and she blinked quickly, looking away from him.

"If you do that, you'd have to tell everyone but Jack to stay away. My pa burned a lot of bridges here in Deadwood, and I'm plum out of skills to rebuild them." She turned and trudged toward her home.

"Mr. Easton! Mr. Easton!" Nancy called as she rushed toward him.

For once, he ignored manners and pretended as if he didn't hear her. He followed Katherine to the edge of town, purposely widening his pace to not only reach Katherine more quickly, but to put more space between himself and Nancy. She'd pestered him all day, and he had no presence of mind left for her.

Katherine crossed her arms and ducked her head as she strode faster. "She's calling for you."

"I think the whole county heard her, but I was already on my way and I didn't plan to stop. If I'm going to walk out to your place, I want to leave enough daylight to walk back home." Thad wished he could wind his hand through Katherine's locked arms and release them, then thread his fingers through hers and show her he not only wasn't ashamed to be seen with her, but wasn't ashamed to be seen giving her his attention. But hearing Nancy behind him stalled his desire.

"Ma isn't feeling well," Katherine mumbled. "She won't be up for company. I didn't want to say anything and make you feel obligated to do something. Because you're always doing something."

He reached out and stopped her, though with her quick pace they were already far outside the city. "I'm sorry to hear that. I don't feel obligated to help you, but I'd like to."

"You've done enough." She stepped out of his reach. "You bought a pistol for me. You gave me a job when no one else in town would. You let me stay even when Mr. Slade told you not to trust me."

He shook his head. "That doesn't account for anything. I'm not even paying you. I could pay you, if that would help." Why did he feel like he was losing her when he was trying so hard to bring her closer?

"No. Like I said, you've done enough."

"I can help you cook. You're tired after a long day, and you'll need to wash up before you can make anything. I didn't do near as much as you did since I had to watch over Miss Powers all day and make certain she didn't injure herself."

Katherine snorted, and he almost laughed at the

sound. He loved that she didn't hide her feelings or reactions. There was nothing fake or genteel about her. If she liked something, she told you. If she didn't, she didn't pretend. Katherine was refreshing.

"I have nothing to offer you," Katherine told him. "We were able to get a few things from the store a few days ago, but we still need meat. I wasn't home all day, so I'll need to grab my rifle when I get home and hunt up some rabbit."

"You have nothing. That's why you didn't bring a meal today."

Katherine's stomach growled loudly to prove him right, and her cheeks turned an even deeper red. A few groceries weren't going to be enough. He had to go to the church as he'd planned and see if they could provide some relief for the entire family. But would interfering make her hate him, or perhaps worse, embarrass her? Hatred she could get over, but often embarrassment never went away.

Thad thought of all the things Nancy had said about Katherine all day, the little comments he'd been loath to correct because he didn't want Nancy to suspect his true feelings for Katherine before he could express them to the woman herself. But if Katherine had heard even part of what had been said, she would assume he agreed since he'd said nothing.

"I didn't realize I'd be here all day," she evaded his statement.

He frowned and changed the subject. "I think you're right about Nancy and the others. Tomorrow we'll have just the three of us. Everyone else can wait until the contest to see what we're up to."

She tilted her head and narrowed her eyes, obviously confused at his choice. "Are you sure we can finish by ourselves?"

Without having to act like someone he wasn't and without having to play nanny to Nancy, he'd get four times the work done. "I absolutely do, and it will be much more peaceful, too." He didn't want to let her go, but if she'd rather walk alone, he'd follow at a distance and alleviate his own mind.

His heart tripped at the smile that spread across her face. That's what he'd been waiting to see all day.

8

Kitty sliced off a fair portion of bread and a sliver of what remained of their butter supply, wrapped it in wax paper, and carefully put it in her lunch pail. She didn't want any sound to wake Ma since she had to leave early to help Thad, and Ma was still in bed.

Thad hadn't followed her all the way home yesterday after he'd finally realized she was worried about what he'd see when he got there. Ma had taken quite a turn, and she looked sickly. Even the boys had stayed away from her, worried that she had something they could catch. Kitty was pretty sure it was catchy and they would get it as soon as they heard from Uncle Damion. Worry could make anyone look like that.

Someone knocked on the door, and Kitty sucked in a breath at the loud sound. She rushed to answer, but Ma slowly puttered from behind the curtain separating her bedroom from the rest of the house. "Who would come so early in the morning?"

Kitty opened the door to Cecil, who gave her a slight nod. "I got this letter for your ma. It says it's urgent, so I rushed it right out here. I didn't know if you'd come to town today or not."

"Thank you," Kitty said as Ma shouldered her out of the way and shut the door the moment Cecil released the letter.

Ma sat down at the table. "Get some coffee brewing." She gently pried open the sticky glue on the paper and unfolded it.

Kitty tried to think of anything good that letter could say, but it was no use. Had someone finally found Pa? Was the letter from Pa? Could Pa even write a letter? Or was the missive from Uncle Damion, finally telling them he wanted repayment for his loan in full?

Her stomach quaked with the idea. Uncle Damion would come and take them all away. She would live in Hot Springs, far away from Deadwood. Far away from Thad. She'd enjoyed seeing him all day yesterday, but watching him interact with the wealthy men of town and with Nancy, she knew her dreams were dust. Despite the letter in the pistol case.

She'd memorized that letter after Thad had treated her so well the evening before, allowing herself to dream about what life with him would be like. But that wasn't meant to be. Even yesterday she'd heard some of what Nancy had said about her, and he hadn't disputed it. In some cases, he'd even chuckled along with Nancy at Kitty's expense.

Kitty recalled the letter again.

She who possesses this pistol possesses an opportunity that must not be squandered. Cast in the tender dreams of maidens from ages past, the steel of this weapon is steadfast and true and will lead an unmarried woman to a man forged from the same virtuous elements. One need only fit her hand to the grip and open her heart to activate the promise for which this pistol was fashioned—the promise of true love. Patience and courage will illuminate her path. Hope and faith will guide her steps until her heart finds its home.

Once the promise is fulfilled, the bearer must release the pistol and pass it to another or risk losing what she has found.

Accept the gift…or not.

Believe its promise…or not.

But hoard the pistol for personal gain…and lose what you hold most dear.

That first line had given her hope. *An opportunity.* She'd never had that before. Trouble was, now she was missing some of that hope and faith. Maybe Pa had pounded them out of her without ever actually having laid a fist to her.

"Girl, you need to promise me something." Ma's murmur forced the air from Kitty's lungs.

"Anything. You know that."

"Win that elite contest. Make your shots count. That money is all that will save this family. The letter is from your uncle. I won't read the whole mess to you, but he's insisting that all of us come and stay with him since your pa can't repay the debt now. We must work for him for seven years to not only pay back what your dad owes, but to pay living expenses during that time, too. I'll never live that long. Not with him." Ma splayed her hand over the letter and closed her eyes.

Kitty stood, rooted to her spot. If she didn't win, her family would suffer for at least seven years. And knowing her uncle like she did, he wouldn't let them go even after that. Maybe he'd let her brothers go, but she and Ma would be stuck with him forever. If she won the contest, she'd hurt Thad. She'd known that was a possibility when she'd had Jack sign up for her, but that was before she'd held that pink pistol. Now, she didn't want to hurt Thad.

Thad would be judged for losing to her. He would be judged for being seen with her. If she were to win the contest, while her family would be safe from harm, her heart would break at losing him.

"Girl, promise." Ma held out a shaky hand.

Love or not, she couldn't let Ma down. Kitty slipped her fingers through her mother's chilly ones. "I promise."

Thad glanced out the narrow window of his office, the dark street ahead offering little as a view. He hadn't meant to be sneaky and to follow Katherine, but he'd wanted to make certain she made it home.

What he'd witnessed there had filled his thoughts and had even kept him from making supper for himself. He hadn't been hungry; he'd been disgusted.

How could a family who lived just outside of a town where money flowed so freely, be let to live in such poverty? Even with the little he'd given them, the meal Katherine's brothers had made would barely be enough to feed him alone, much less feed six of them. No wonder Katherine was like a willow tree.

Worse, Katherine still hadn't signed up for the women's shooting competition, leaving people asking him after her. He wasn't sure what to tell them, not after what he'd seen.

Her mother had looked desperately ill from the little he could see. She'd hobbled outside to sit on the front porch as Katherine had come home, the woman having deteriorated quickly in the few days since he'd seen her.

Thad paced to the other end of his small office and turned, tucking his arms behind his back. He needed to think and think quickly.

Jack knocked softly on the doorjamb. "You sent for me?"

"I did. I need your help right away."

Jack held out his hand. "Let's dispense with the 'right away' fee."

Thad dug in his wallet and handed the boy a nickel. "Go, get Preacher Fielding. I need to talk to him."

"This is about Kitty, isn't it? You think you fancy her."

Thad didn't think, he knew, but he wasn't about to argue the matter with a boy. "If it makes you go any faster, yes, it's about her."

Instead of leaving, Jack stepped farther into the room and closed the door. "You can't help her. The town won't let you. As soon as you give her something, someone else will show up to claim it as theirs. I know how this works. I've lived on the street for five years."

Thad had wondered about Jack and how he'd grown so wise in so short a time. "People steal from you?"

"If you let them, and she's too nice not to let them. She won't see it coming, and they'll leave her with even less than she had before. Do her a favor and leave her alone. If you start paying attention, so will other people."

"People like Nancy."

"And Slade," Jack fairly growled.

"The banker?"

"He's the worst of them all. I'd saved up money from working at the livery. I was so proud to finally have a job that I didn't really consider all that it meant. I tucked away all my savings in a little cigar box in the straw where I would bed down for the night. I saved up ten whole dollars. Do you know how long it takes to save that much when you're twelve?" He let out a long breath.

"I went into the bank, thinking I was a man. I was going to start an account and have a safe place to keep my money. Slade saw me coming and waved me into his office. He smiled and congratulated me. He told me how proud he was that I was making the choice to become a real man."

Thad didn't miss the sheen of tears in the boy's eyes at recalling the tale. Shame was hard to swallow. "And he stole it from you?"

"Just as bad. He had me sign a form saying that I had an account with the bank, then he told me I owed him fifteen dollars to set it up."

Thad's jaw dropped, and he couldn't believe what he was hearing. Fifteen dollars was almost two weeks' wages for a hard worker. There was no way he would charge that much just to open an account.

"When I told him I didn't have that much, he laughed and said that I'd signed the form. I had to pay. He said he'd go talk to my boss and have the money sent to him directly."

"So you quit and haven't had a steady job since."

Jack swiped the back of his hand across his nose. "Exactly. Slade can't collect what he can't see. He won't cheat me again. And he did cheat me. I asked Cecil how much he had to pay for his bank account. He said he didn't pay anything for the bank to hold his money. He just had to pay for other services, like printing cheques."

Thad had never thought Slade was that dirty. The idea turned his stomach. "So, you're worried that if I take notice of the Horwath family—if I try to help them out—they'll end up in a worse state than they are now?"

"All I'm saying is, before I sat in that office with

the shiny leather chairs and the polished floors, I was earning a steady income and proud of what I was doing. I left that office feeling like I could never hold a job again."

The livery owner had recently sold to a new man in town, Thad thought. Maybe that was Jack's ticket. "That livery owner's gone now. You could start over."

Jack shook his head and headed for the door. "I'll go get that preacher for you and you can do all you want, but don't forget what I told you. Mark my words, she'll pay for your help, and Kitty doesn't deserve that." He opened the door and walked away.

Thad had to agree. Kitty deserved to be protected from the likes of vermin who would take advantage, but how could he do that? He could barely talk to her without her shutting him out. Tomorrow when they worked he'd ask her what her family needed most. Food was essential, but if he could give them security somehow, then he would.

He thought about the five-dollar prize for the women's competition. That wouldn't make a bit of difference. Not in the long run. He needed to do better, and fast.

9

T had stood in a small group of men outside the church, warming themselves in the sun and talking about the coming contest. After working with Katherine and Jack the day before, he'd almost managed the entire setup, which was good because the lumberyard needed him.

Katherine crossed the street about three blocks away from the church along with her brothers, but their Ma was nowhere to be seen. He'd hoped the whole family would come that day so he could have the food, clothing, and ammunition he'd purchased for them delivered to their house without incident. Now Katherine's ma would harass the poor boy he'd hired to deliver the goods. For the first time in a long time, he hadn't hired Jack to do the errand.

Jack's words had hit him hard, and he'd begun to look differently at the men who, by virtue of their bank accounts and prestige, ran the town. If those men didn't like a man, that man wouldn't succeed. Thad's own success could be measured because he'd become friends and allies with those men. But Jack was an outsider, as was Katherine and her family.

So, Thad had decided to bring Jack into the fold, but he had to do it slowly and carefully. Starting with a job that was scheduled, consistent, and put Jack in a place to prove he was honest. Which meant the lumberyard had a new sales position. The boy carried himself as if he were much older than his seventeen years, so Thad would make it work. He'd start Jack with just a few accounts, then steadily give him more work.

But the very first thing he'd do was right the wrong that had been done at the bank. Slade would never try to pull the wool over Thad's eyes like he'd done to Jack. Even now, the boy refused to go to church with Thad because he'd have to see the man who'd duped him. It didn't put Jack in a mind to thank God when he wanted justice.

Katherine straightened her spine as she approached the group of men. She had to know most of them didn't approve of her. Thad hoped she also knew that he didn't feel the same.

"Miss Katherine? A word with you?" Thad stepped away from the group so he wouldn't have to see their looks of surprise or sounds of disapproval.

Her glance darted all around. "Now?"

"If we could? Let's step just over there so I could speak to you." He pointed toward the large spruce tree at the edge of the church's front lawn. "I'll only keep you a moment."

She shooed her brothers away. "Alex, I'll meet you inside."

"Yes, ma'am." Alex snickered slightly, and Katherine pinched his ear before he could duck away to the safety of the church.

Katherine trudged alongside Thad, smelling fresh without any hint of false fragrances or expensive toilette water. He wondered momentarily if she would like some, then tossed aside the idea. While Katherine might appreciate a mildly scented rose soap, he doubted she would ever use it for anything but special occasions. She just wasn't a girl who liked frippery.

"What is it? Have I done something wrong?" Katherine crossed her arms over her ecru dress that had been in fashion before he was old enough to care about women's dresses.

"Absolutely not." He smiled, trying to relieve some of the tension in her stiff shoulders. "As much as I've enjoyed working with you, we're almost finished putting the contest site together. I won't need you to come until the day before to help me finish. Once we kept out the riffraff, finishing didn't take long."

She finally smiled at him. "I was worried I'd done something wrong and would need to go fix it. I was glad to help."

Thad turned around, and all of the men he'd just left behind quickly turned back together in a bunch, pretending they hadn't been watching him.

"They surely have nothing better to do." Katherine gave a long sigh.

"I can't figure out why they seem so intent on watching you and Jack."

She frowned, then shook her head. "If you think it's just me and Jack, then you haven't opened your eyes. It's anyone outside of their little group. And invitations to join are rare."

Especially if they saw those outside of their group as targets to exploit. Did she count him among them? "I hope you know I wouldn't do that to you."

Katherine slowly shook her head and laid a gentle hand on his arm, sending a confounding feeling straight through his coat and shirt all the way to his skin, and zinging right to his chest. He froze, wanting her to stay there and afraid that if he even breathed she'd flit away.

"I know you wouldn't," she replied. "You've been nothing but kind and generous. I don't know how I'll ever repay you. I probably won't be able to."

He hoped she saw something worthwhile in her future. Surely she had some hope. "Don't worry about any such thing. I don't want repayment. I just want to see you happy." At least he could be completely honest about that.

The church bell clanged, warning them the service would start shortly. "One last thing," he said. He still didn't move, and her hand lingered on his arm as if she didn't want to let him go any more than he wanted her to stay.

"Yes?"

"I noticed your roof was looking very worn, and Alex might not know how to repair it. I have some shingles that were sitting outside and are a weathered gray. They are still good, but no one will buy them. Can I come over tomorrow afternoon and fix your roof? I'd like to teach Alex how to do it."

Katherine's jaw dropped, and she finally pulled back. "I...don't think that's a good idea."

SPRING WOULD BRING fluke rainstorms over the mountains, and Kitty's family would get wet. Maybe. If they were still there. Uncle Damion hadn't arrived yet, but Ma didn't send him a reply to his letter, so Kitty knew he would come. He could be there even now, and Ma was all alone in the house.

"Do you have another way to fix it?" Thad continued the conversation with her. "I know your ma doesn't like charity, but this would be doing me a favor. I can't put out new shingles until these are gone. You need shingles, I need to get rid of those I have." He shifted his hands up and down like weights on a scale. "Seems to me that giving you what I have in order to help me do what I need to do, is a good thing. That isn't charity. It's good business."

"You know Ma won't see it that way," Kitty said, gnawing on her lip and wishing she could dash off inside the church where she wouldn't have to answer questions about Ma.

With the hardship of knowing Uncle Damion was

coming, Ma was getting worse. She could barely walk, and she couldn't eat. The coffee she'd cursed just days before was now the only thing she could keep in her stomach.

"I don't think Alex is in any state to learn," Kitty continued. Not that he didn't want to do all the things men were supposed to know how to do, though. Pa had never bothered to teach Alex anything but trapping, a skill he didn't use at all.

"Katherine, I know you're worried about your ma. But it needs to be done, and there's no other way to do it."

Kitty hated feeling like she had no choice in the matter. Last year, when Pa had been there, he'd ignored the leaks and put Ma's pans all around the house to catch the water. He'd told the younger boys to empty them when they needed emptying. That wasn't a solution she really wanted to reuse.

"I know you're right, but I don't have to like it," Kitty said. After all, having him there would put even more strain on Ma. How Thad saw what he was doing and how Ma saw it would be two different things, and there would be no way to change Ma's mind.

"Think about it during the service, then come find me and let me know afterward." The final bell chimed, and she glanced around, realizing they were standing on the lawn alone.

"That's a good idea. We'd best get inside."

Thad nodded his agreement and headed for the door, then held it open for her. She'd never had anyone do that for her except her brothers. Men didn't see her as a woman, so they didn't think manners mattered with her. Thad treated everyone with respect and manners. Money or not.

Kitty dashed along the back of the church and slid into the aisle where her family always sat just as the preacher went to the front. Alex elbowed her and scowled a silent warning. She'd get an earful on the walk home. He didn't even like coming to church and certainly didn't like sitting there alone with his brothers.

She mouthed the word *sorry* silently, and he shook his head. The discussion wasn't over. That much she knew. But how could she decide what to do without talking to Alex? There wouldn't be time for talking.

Inside her mother's Bible, as worn as it was, was a folded sheet Ma used to write verses that the preacher used in his sermons so she could look them up later. Kitty took the nub of a pencil from the holder in the back of the pew in front of her and wrote on the paper:

Thad wants to come fix our roof, teach you to do it, and he'll provide shingles.

Alex glanced at her with one raised brow. He was just as suspicious as she usually was. But this was Thad. He wasn't going to turn on them or do something for his own gain.

Her brother leaned close and whispered softly, "Why would we fix the house when we may only be living there for another week, maybe two?"

She didn't think she could meter her voice like Alex, so she gripped the pencil once more and wrote:

Because it's the right thing to do for whoever owns the place after us.

There was no hope of paying off the debt. She'd tried to get a job in Deadwood, and Thad had been the only one who had hired her, and even that was only for a few days and to pay for the pistol. He hadn't offered her a paying job when she'd asked.

Alex shook his head and turned his focus to the front. The preacher probably had something good to say, but she couldn't listen. Her mind focused too much on Thad's offer and the fact that she had to answer him right after the preacher finished.

When the service ended, Alex stood and dashed for the door along with the others, leaving Kitty in the pew alone. Nancy stood six pews ahead, her nose in the air. Her new dress fit her perfectly. She made her way toward Thad and laid a hand on his arm as she spoke to him. He smiled at her, but it was different from the smile he'd given to Kitty, though she couldn't explain how. It just *felt* different.

Ma had wanted Kitty to think about the letter inside the pink-pistol box. She'd felt this was a chance Kitty couldn't pass up. Thad hadn't come around at all until that pistol came to town, and now Kitty saw him almost daily. Maybe she'd give the words in that funny letter a chance.

Nancy or not, Kitty strode over to where Thad stood talking. She waited her turn, even when Nancy moved to stand right in front of her and kept talking to Thad.

"Nancy, it was good talking to you, but I need to have a word with Katherine. Excuse me," Thad said.

Kitty couldn't help feeling her chest swell with pride—as evil as she knew that was, especially in the house of God—when Nancy *harumphed* and walked away.

"So, what's your decision?" Thad's eyes gleamed, challenging her to accept his offer.

"I guess I'll see you tomorrow afternoon."

10

At receiving the word Thad would be coming to fix the roof, Ma's health suddenly improved enough to come and sit in her chair in the kitchen. She rolled potatoes toward herself and quickly peeled them while Kitty scrubbed the kitchen floor.

"I didn't ever find out who sent that wagonload of goods yesterday. It's like the supply wagon for the mercantile went to the wrong place." She slid the knife from one end of the potato to the other with a flick of her wrist.

Kitty had a pretty good idea who'd sent the items, but she couldn't say for sure. Knowing how Ma felt about gifts made her keep her mouth shut. "It was surely kind of someone, and I'm grateful I don't have to go hunting for our supper tonight when I have a house to clean. We haven't had an expected guest in a long time."

"Too long. Your pa never considered that you'd be courting soon."

Thank goodness she was on her knees and up to her elbows in hot water so Ma didn't see the heat warming her cheeks. She was most certainly *not* courting. Though if Thad asked her to join them in fixing the roof, she wouldn't say no. If that was courting, then she'd concede they were.

She scrubbed in small circles over the bare floor. No man had ever come to call. Not all through school. Not after school. Not when she'd passed the age Pa would've needed to give his approval. Not even when he'd left and that barrier was completely gone.

No man in Deadwood made her feel like Thad did, but he was far above her station. Truly, she should be looking toward the young men who worked at the livery or maybe some of the few farmers in the area.

"Best go dump that water. He'll be here shortly, and you don't want to be down there scrubbing when he knocks on the door."

While Ma was right, the floor didn't look as nice as she'd wanted it to. Thad would come inside for supper, and he hadn't been given the best impression the first time when the kitchen had been full of steam from her coffee mishap.

"I'll do that, but I'll get some fresh water the moment he climbs the ladder to the roof. Where's Alex?"

"I'm not sure," Ma replied. "I know he was around back last I saw him. He was looking forward to learning, so I don't think he'd go far." Ma set the final potato in a large enamel bowl and stood, stretching her back. "I'll go see if I can find him."

Kitty lugged the wash bucket out back, carrying it farther from the house than she normally would, so there wouldn't be a mud puddle right out the back door. While it was unlikely Thad would go out that door, the shingles on the house were worse on the back, and the mere possibility made her wax cautious.

"Alex?" Ma called from the back door as Kitty swung the now empty bucket on her way back to the house.

Kitty's new boots still surprised her when they peeked out from under her hems. In the pile of goods left the day before, there had been enough food to fill their storage area, some new blankets for the beds, hats for each of the boys, a walking cane for Ma, and a pair of boots that fit Kitty perfectly. Her own boots had been about ready to lose their soles.

The jingle of traces let her know someone in a wagon was on the way toward the house. Thad was there. Almost certainly. Her heart tripped as she glanced down at herself and yanked the kerchief off her head. Picking up her pace, she rushed through the back door.

Ma had already made it through the house and was just opening the front door as Kitty rushed to her side. There, driving down the lane, was Thad atop a wagon loaded with shingles and supplies. After today, there would be no reason to worry about the roof. Kitty wouldn't have to listen for thunder in the evening and worry.

Thad smiled and waved before he pulled the team to a stop in the front yard. "Good morning!" he called.

"Fine Monday morning," Ma answered. "Do you have all the help you need at the yard?"

He turned around and climbed down, landing in a cloud of dust as his feet hit the gravel of the driveway. "I do. I've recently hired a few men who are good. I trust them." He stood next to the wagon and glanced up toward the roof. "This is sure to take all day. Alex, you ready?"

Alex pushed forward past Kitty. "Yes, sir. I had to find my hat." He flopped it on his head. "Pro'ly going to be hot up there." He wiped his brow as if it were already sweaty.

"Probably, but with your help, we'll get it done quickly. First thing we'll need to do is pull down all the damaged, old shingles."

"Can I help too, Mr. Easton?"

Kitty tried to hold in her surprise as her younger brother Grayson tried to stand as tall next to his brother as he could. At fifteen, he was man enough to go up and help.

"I think that's a great idea. If I'm going to teach one of you, it's a good use of my time to teach both."

Thad shifted his hat slightly, then caught Kitty's eye. Her heart thrummed softly. "Good to see you," he said.

Kitty prayed her heart wasn't showing on her face. "Good to see you, too. If you should need anything at all, let the boys know and they can come find me. There are ladders in the barn."

"Perfect."

She had the strangest feeling he wasn't talking about the ladders.

Thad followed Alex and Grayson toward the old barn at the back of the yard. All around were signs of decay and neglect. Katherine's father hadn't been one to fix things or pick up after working, as evidenced by the tools laying around in various places and partially finished projects dotting the yard.

A goat bleated near a small shed where it tugged on a small chain.

"That's Fred. Pa threatened to shoot him if he didn't stay out of the house, so we had to put him on a chain out here." Grayson bounded over to the little thing and held his hand out, palm up. At the sight, the goat lowered its chin and charged the boy, ramming his little rack square into the boy's palm.

Grayson laughed and patted the little billy on the head. The encouragement made the goat jump and bleat all the more.

"I didn't know you had any livestock out here." Thad turned his attention back to the barn to look for the ladders.

"We don't. Not really." Alex scratched his chin. "I mean, there's the goat. We have three sheep that just appeared here one morning and none of the farmers around here said they were missing any. We have one old horse who only pulls the wagon when she wants, and one younger horse who never wants to. That's why we only take the wagon when we have to."

Thad recalled seeing Alex driving Katherine in town, and he agreed with her younger brother's assessment. Even the younger horse didn't want to pull. Both horses were in the barn currently, and Thad realized they had no fence in which to roam. They had to live their whole lives in a pen when they weren't pulling.

"Did your pa own this place?" he asked the boys. Though he doubted either boy knew anything about ownership of the property.

"Nope," Grayson replied. "My uncle owns it, and Pa was trying to buy it from him. Uncle Damion got Pa to ask for a loan when there was a big dust-up after the fire in Deadwood. Pa lost all his traps and things, and he needed to replace them. That was before I was born though. I think Kitty was only four."

"I was only just born." Alex shifted a few old cans around, then handed Thad a container of roofing nails.

"Thank you." Thad had brought some, but if they had supplies, he'd use them. "How long has your dad been gone?"

Alex scratched his chin. "Odd thing that I don't recall exactly. Pa leaves a lot, so when he took off, I didn't much notice. I figured he'd be back in a day or two with a bunch of stories and some pelts."

"But then Pa never came home," Grayson mumbled.

Thad hefted two ladders at once toward the house. A rock formed in his gut that he didn't want to think about. He'd hoped he could talk to Slade at the bank about keeping up on any payments Katherine's pa might have had left, but if her uncle owned the house he couldn't.

"Will your uncle come to stay with you?" Thad asked.

Both Alex and Grayson wrinkled their noses. "I sure hope not. He's horrible," Alex said, taking one ladder from Thad and leaning it against the roof. "Let's get to work!"

There were only a few areas of the roof that were really bad and had probably needed repair for years. Since he had the help of Katherine's brothers and they seemed to crave his attention and time, Thad decided early on to do more than was needed. There was more help to be given than just a new roof.

"Pa never would've shown us how to do this. I knew it needed doing but didn't have the know-how. Thank you, Mr. Easton." Alex had pounded in the small nails like a carpenter after just a few tries. The boy had the knack.

"I'm glad to help, and you can call me Thad." He'd told them a few times already, but they didn't seem to feel comfortable enough to do that yet. "You're both doing so well, you'll have to come see me for jobs when you come of age." Assuming he wasn't run out of town for consorting with Katherine. Slade had caught on to his plan to work with Katherine alone—though Jack had been there. Slade had told Thad in no uncertain terms that Katherine would never be trusted. Her family was garbage and would never rise above what they were.

Thad realized if he chose to court Katherine, he was also courting his own disaster.

He glanced across the patches of new shingles scattered among the old, tattered ones. "I've got enough shingles here to do the whole roof, but I don't have time to come out here every day. It won't be easy to work around what we've already done, but I think you both could do it."

Grayson grinned over at Thad. "I think you're right, and it'll make Ma happy. But…what about Uncle Damion?"

"Grayson, hush."

Thad glanced between the two boys, but both their jaws had firmed to stony silence. "Let's climb down and see what that wonderful smell is." He'd been catching whiffs of some type of meat and definitely potatoes. Every once in a while the breeze would be just right, sending the luscious scent of bread to his nose. His stomach growled. After being on the roof all day with the exception of a short break at noon for a quick sandwich, he was famished.

Mrs. Horwath sat at the table. Every place was ready, but he wasn't sure where he should sit, so he delayed the decision by heading to the washbasin to freshen his face and hands. On a usual day, he didn't get particularly dirty unless there wasn't anyone else around to do the physical labor. He'd done that work for a few years and now gladly paid others. However, today fixing the roof and accomplishing something with his hands felt good.

Katherine had changed into a nicer dress than she'd been wearing when he'd arrived, and he noticed the boots he'd bought peeking out from her hems as she bustled about bringing food to the table. He made himself useful and helped her bring the last few things.

A bowl with beans waited near the stove, and he reached to grab it at the same moment Katherine did. She froze with the bowl between them, her eyes locked with his. Something passed between them, and for a moment there was only the two of them in the kitchen, like they'd done this a thousand times.

"Supper smells wonderful," he said, giving her what he hoped was a warm smile, but he felt silly, like he was trying too hard.

Katherine let go of the bowl and brushed her hair behind her ear. "I've been cooking with Ma since I was nine. I can cook almost as well as I can shoot."

If that were true, he was in for a treat. Since he already felt silly, he didn't say what he was thinking. He was absolutely certain anything that smelled this wonderful had to taste good.

After the most satisfying meal he'd had in years, Thad sat enjoying a mug of coffee with Mrs. Horwath and Katherine. The boys had cleared the table and finished the dishes. They'd left to play out back but were strictly told not to torment the poor goat.

"Now, Thad, Kitty tells me you're running that

shooting contest again this year. What are we building with all the proceeds?" Ma asked.

Thad hadn't had much opportunity to talk with anyone but Slade about the roller rink, but it excited him. "I have approval to build a roller-skating rink just outside of town. I'm hoping to give the young people something to do that has nothing to do with gambling, drinking, or"—he'd forgotten his company and his manners for just a moment—"other things."

Mrs. Horwath cackled. "We certainly need to keep them away from other things. I'm so glad Kitty got the opportunity to work with you."

"Ma, I told you, I'm just working to pay him back for that pistol." Katherine's cheeks went pink in the soft light of the candle at the center of the table. Thad couldn't stop looking at her, not that he tried overly hard.

"Consider the pistol paid for, though I never asked you to repay me. But I have enjoyed working with you," Thad said. *Careful, she might catch on to how you feel...*

With a stifled yawn, Mrs. Horwath stood. "It's been quite the long day for everyone. I'm going to retire to my room. Kitty, see Mr. Easton out, but you mind yourself." She shook her finger at Katherine, but the gleam in her eye gave her away.

"I will mind my manners, Mrs. Horwath," Thad said. "Thank you for having me to supper."

Ma gave him a brief smile and nod before she headed for her room, leaning on the cane he'd made sure was in the wagon the day before. They were using everything he'd provided, which filled him with joy. If only other people like him would try giving to those in need instead of trying to keep people in poverty, maybe they would experience joy, too.

Katherine strolled alongside him back to his wagon. The boys had hitched his horses, who patiently waited for him to take them back to the livery for the evening. He stood beside the wagon, wanting the moment to last much longer than it would.

When else would he get time with Katherine, alone, with the sun setting in the distance? Her hair was like spun gold in the rays of sunlight. Birds chirped their evening goodnight in the trees, and the heat of the day had melted to a cool evening.

"Thank you for fixing our roof. You keep doing all of these things, and there's just no way I can pay you back." Katherine crossed her arms over her stomach.

Thad hated that the woman he'd always known as strong and self-sufficient felt unsure when it came to him. "You don't need to. I don't want you to ever feel like you need to pay back a gift. I see you using the things I've given you, and that makes me utterly happy." He drew closer to her. "Being with you and your family makes me happy."

She tilted her chin up to look at him, and he was lost. Would her skin be soft? Would her hair? He had to find out. Without considering the ramifications, he cupped her cheek. She gasped softly but didn't pull away from him.

His lips found hers as he wondered over their softness and confirmed that they were the softest part of her yet. She made a slight noise in her throat, and he relaxed, preparing to step aside, and praying she didn't slap him, though he probably deserved it.

Instead, she wrapped her arms around his neck and pulled him closer. However, having Katherine flush against him reminded him of every reason he couldn't stay here kissing her in the breezy dim light of the evening. He had to be an upright man and do this the right way.

He stepped back, brushing her mussed hair from her face. "Thank you for a wonderful day."

Her lips were dark and slightly parted as she nodded her agreement. For once, he'd left Katherine Horwath speechless.

11

Ma sat next to Kitty the next morning humming a jaunty tune of praise. She pulled the plate of eggs toward her and took two scoops, more than she'd eaten in the morning for days.

"You're feeling better then?" Kitty handed Ma the salt and pepper bowls.

"Much. I finally feel like we have some hope. With Thad as our ally and with the shooting competition money, we may have enough to keep our home. What if your pa came back and we weren't here?" Ma's eyes glistened.

Kitty wasn't sure how Ma could still care about Pa after all he'd done, but somehow she did. Her thoughts returned to Thad's kiss from the night before. That kiss had kept her awake, but not with hope.

Thad was certainly interested in her, but would he still be after he found out she'd lied to him and entered the elite competition? Ma had sworn her to silence about the threat of Uncle Damion, and the boys had to swear as well. Ma didn't want Thad to do anything out of obligation.

"What if I don't win?" Kitty pushed her own plate away, no longer hungry.

"Of course you'll win!" Alex chimed in. "You're the best shot there is."

"That's pride and a sin," Kitty mumbled. "Maybe you should do the contest for me."

Ma narrowed her eyes and remained silent just long enough for Kitty to squirm. "I know you think you mean well, but Alex is too young. As good of a shot as he is, he's not you."

Which meant Kitty would have to put her family above her growing feelings for Thad. Even with the prediction of the pistol's note, love couldn't grow from a lie. And even if she found a dollar to enter in the women's competition now, the prize wouldn't be enough to pay back Uncle Damion. He'd still come and take them away. And since Pa had left their land such a mess, her uncle would probably sell everything off, leaving her nothing to return to after the seven years.

Assuming he'd truly let them go after that time.

Kitty opened her mouth, but the confession wouldn't come. And if she couldn't tell Ma, how could she tell Thad? He'd told her how he had to be careful with his reputation or he might lose his business. While people wouldn't back out of attending the event because of her—since they couldn't know the false name on the list was her—Thad and Amos could drop out of the competition. If they did, she wouldn't win anything. The rules stated that in order to win, the shooter had to actually hit the target *against* another shooter.

Even if Thad agreed to shoot against her, winning against him would make him a laughingstock. He wouldn't ever do anything to hurt her, but in order to help her family, she would have to hurt him.

Kitty stood and scraped her plate into the scrap pail for the goat, then headed to her room. The case for the pink pistol sat closed on her dresser. She opened it and touched the cold metal of the barrel. Were there others who had owned the gun who'd failed to find love? Surely she wasn't the only one to own it who had done something to ruin her chances.

She tugged the thick paper from its hiding spot and glanced over the letter and the names again. There were some time spans where there weren't names written, though perhaps those people simply hadn't wanted to be known. Would she be the first to write on the paper that she'd failed?

And if she did, would she break whatever wonderful gift came with the gun? Her skin chilled, and she tucked the letter away, then closed the lid. No pink-pistol love prediction was going to make what she'd done better. She had to tell Thad and let him decide what to do since she didn't have months to work for the money. Uncle Damion would be coming soon.

"Katherine, get out here right now." Ma's voice brooked no argument.

Kitty didn't bother to answer as she rushed back to the kitchen. An automobile drove steadily up the lane. The driver was a large man, roughly looking like Pa but more robust, and Pa would never drive an automobile.

"Uncle Damion."

"Yes. I'm going to try to convince him to let you shoot in that competition. I'll think of some reason. You have to win. If you don't, he'll own us for the rest of our lives. He has the money to convince a judge he's doing us a favor, if I could ever get a judge to hear a case against him. No one will believe he's doing anything wrong."

Jack had told her all wealthy people were out to get poor people, to take advantage of them. Her uncle was no exception. Thad was different, but she couldn't tell him what Uncle Damion was going to do. Her heart might break if he didn't believe her. Getting away from Uncle Damion was more important than her infatuation with Thad. Perhaps if she won and sent her uncle back home empty-handed, she could tell Thad what she'd done to be in the contest. He might even forgive her.

The automobile stopped out front, and the silence seemed louder than the car as Kitty watched her uncle lumber from behind the steering wheel and come around to the door. He didn't bother to knock and walked right in, catching them all in the act of staring at him.

"Well, if it isn't my brother's family. When was the last time you saw him?" He took off his hat and hung it on Pa's peg by the door.

Ma lost all color as she brought her empty plate to the washbasin. "It's been a few months."

"Months? My brother has been missing for that long, and you didn't think it was necessary to let me know? Didn't you think I might want to get paid?" He shrugged out of his greatcoat and hung that on the coat-tree.

"He spent plenty of time gone in the past few years. I had no reason to believe he wouldn't return." Ma turned her back to Uncle Damion and began scrubbing the dishes.

Kitty stood back watching the scene, ready to stand between him and her ma if he did anything. She wouldn't shoot him, but he didn't know that. She waited until Alex met her gaze, then she subtly ticked her head to the side, motioning for the boys to leave.

The boys didn't wait for their uncle to stop them and dashed out the back. At least the boys wouldn't hear what needed to be said. "I don't agree with your plan in your letter. I think we can get the money for you. You just have to be willing to wait," Kitty said, straightening her spine and forcing a calm threat into her voice that she didn't feel.

"I don't have to do anything. I own this house. Now that my brother isn't here to protect all of you, you need me." He narrowed his eyes at her. "I stopped in town to talk to Mr. Slade. I needed to see if my brother had any other loans or outstanding debts. At least the man had enough sense not to borrow what he couldn't repay from anyone but me."

That was perhaps the one thing she could agree her pa had done right by his family. Ma set the last plate aside to dry and turned around to face her brother-in-law. "I won't willingly go with you until after the shooting contest. Kitty helped the organizer set it up, and he'll wonder what happened to us if we're not there."

"The organizer? Who's that?" Damion looked at Kitty with utter contempt.

"Mr. Easton, owner of the lumberyard."

Uncle Damion drummed his fingers on the table. "I don't see any reason to wait. I've come all this way, and I don't want to dawdle here."

"Kitty has a commitment, and you've always said that Aspen wasn't a man of his word. Kitty is. You make her the very thing you hate by taking her away." Ma stood tall, though her skirts quivered slightly with her fatigue.

Kitty wanted to get Ma's cane and give it to her, but that would make Ma seem weak to Damion, and that would never do. "I do," Kitty said. "I've signed my name and given my word."

"Your word means nothing. You're Aspen Horwath's daughter."

"She is working to change all that," Ma said. "If we're supposed to work for you for seven years, we have to think about our lives after that. We have to have built something—a name for ourselves—to return to."

Damion snorted, but didn't contradict Ma. Though Kitty doubted he ever planned to give them back their freedom. "You can take my room," Kitty told him. "I just need to move a few things in with Ma, and I'll stay there." Then he couldn't say they'd cost him more money by having him stay at the hotel in town.

"Fine. You can shoot in the competition. Be ready to leave directly after." He turned and headed outside.

Ma immediately collapsed into the chair, her breathing haggard. "We can't leave with him. We can't. Your father wasn't a great man, but he was better than Damion by any measure imaginable. You have to win that competition, Kitty. If you don't, I don't know that we'll ever have a say in anything again."

12

Kitty's heart whispered in her ear to tell the truth. She'd learned in church that Jesus wanted her to be honest all the time. Even when it didn't feel good. He'd certainly gone through a lot that didn't feel good. And not telling the truth felt a lot like not trusting the Lord.

But therein lay the problem. She struggled with trust. Especially when the fate of her family rested on her shoulders. The Israelites survived slavery, but she doubted they were happy about it. In fact, most of the time, they cried out to the Lord when they were enslaved. Now as Kitty neared town, she still didn't have a clear picture in her mind of what to do.

The noisy mill for the lumberyard saws sat at the end of town, and for some reason, walking the distance felt a lot longer than usual. Just as Kitty walked by the café, Nancy came out of it and laughed.

"Would you look at Kitty Horwath?" She leaned in close to the friend standing next to her. "Wonder if she's on her way to the pawnbroker to give him whatever she can scrounge together to pay her fee. Maybe this is the year someone else wins." She laughed again.

Kitty focused on the street ahead of her. Maybe if she didn't give Nancy the attention she so desperately wanted, Nancy would leave her be.

"Hey, diddle, diddle…" Nancy dissolved into giggles.

With renewed focus, Kitty rushed farther down the street, her cheeks flaming. Children had mocked her with that nursery rhyme the moment she'd started school as a child because her mother had called her Kitty from the moment she was born. No matter how little sense they made in saying it, she still hated it.

In a rush, she shoved open the door to the lumberyard and came face-to-face with Jack, dressed in his best clothes and working.

"Kitty!" He smiled. "Would you look at this? I'm working!"

While he usually didn't show his age, today he truly looked seventeen in his exuberance to have a job.

"Good for you!" She wished she could say the same. Thad had never offered her work for pay.

Thad came out from his office carrying a long rolled sheet of paper. He saw Kitty and his face softened into a smile. "I didn't think I'd get to see you today. Come back into my office. We can talk."

She'd never been invited to his office before. Kitty gave Jack what she hoped was a reassuring smile and then followed Thad through the door to his office. She left it open for the sake of propriety and sat in the chair he offered in front of his desk.

"I'm so glad you came in. I just got the plans for the roller rink. Do you want to see them?"

She couldn't deny him his excitement. He'd worked so hard. Would taking a minute to show him some enthusiasm hurt her? Quickly swallowing her need to confess everything right away before she lost her nerve, she forced a smile. "I'd love to see them."

Odd that Thad didn't worry about fumbling the huge pages in front of Mr. Slade or anyone else, but the worry immediately hit him that he didn't want Katherine to see him as a bumbling oaf. He carefully unrolled the sheet, anchoring it on one end with the paper weight on top of his desk and with his pencil holder on the other.

Just looking over the plans invigorated him. This roller rink would be a place for young and old to relax and enjoy themselves. If Deadwood was going to continue to grow, it needed places like this.

Katherine slid to the edge of her seat and craned her neck to look at the page. "I'm not certain what I'm seeing."

He invited her to stand next to him, and she slowly

came around the desk. She carried a fresh scent on her today of spruce, like she'd been walking through the trees all day until she'd found herself in his office. He leaned over the desk to focus on the page, not the woman.

"Here is the round floor made of varnished wood where the skaters will go round and round. Here is the counter where people will be able to rent skates for a few cents. There will be tables to talk and rest along this side. Can you picture it?"

She stared down at the squares and circles on the sheet, then slowly nodded her head. "If I try, I surely can. Though I've never been on skates in my life. Not even ice skates."

Building the rink would take time, but he wanted to see Katherine enjoy the building just as much as everyone else. "When it's completed, do you want to go?"

She took a step back. "I don't think I'd belong in there. Put wheels on my feet and I'm liable to fall."

The thought that she might be as unsure or nervous around him as he was around her made his heart race a little faster. "We would all have to learn. Not a one of us is used to that sort of thing."

She flushed slightly. "Are you telling me all those wealthy people don't have roller rinks in their sitting parlors?"

She'd never teased him before, and even though she could easily be talking about him—since he fit in with those people—he got the sense she thought differently of him, and that pleased him. "None that I know of." He laughed.

Katherine paled slightly and turned toward the window. "I'm sure it will all be great fun. I don't think I'll be able to go, but I hope you enjoy it completely."

He needed to touch her, to comfort her from her worry. He would take care of her. Even if he had to continue to do so in secret, though he'd rather lavish her with gifts out in the open. He followed her to the window and laid his hands on her arms, feeling her tense and pull in a breath.

"I want to experience the rink *with* you, Katherine."

KITTY'S HEART RACED. She wanted to lean back and melt into his embrace, to let him take care of all her problems and the weight of her family obligations, but that was impossible. Because she couldn't tell him. If she told him she was registered under a man's name, he would have to be honest with all those men who'd donated money so far and those who'd purchased tickets. The same tickets that would pay for the rink the town so desperately needed.

She would have to let Ma down and pray her uncle would let her and her older brothers work for him while Ma and the two younger boys stayed on in Deadwood or lived with him if he wanted to sell the house. Ma could do very little anyway.

She stepped away from Thad's intoxicating touch

and gathered her wits about her. She couldn't allow him to get any closer to her knowing she would be leaving in a week. Right after the contest—the one she would now forfeit—she would be leaving town. For good.

13

T had watched confounded as Katherine quickly made her excuses and practically ran from his office. He followed to see where she'd go, but she ducked in an alley a few blocks away and he didn't want her thinking he was chasing her.

What had he done? He'd merely said he wanted to spend time with her. She had been the one to come see him, but try as he might, he couldn't recall her stating why. He'd like to believe she wanted to simply spend time with him, but the way she'd dashed off proved that was not the case.

He came back inside, drawing Jack into his office and offering him a seat, then rolled up the plans. Asking Jack anything about Katherine could lead to more questions than he wanted to state out loud, but Jack was one of the few people Katherine confided in.

"Did Katherine happen to say anything to you when she came in? She left quickly, without stating why she was here. I wondered if I misunderstood her reason for coming to the mill. Perhaps she came to see you?" Thad clenched his teeth tightly to say no more. The more he said, the more he would give away.

Jack slowly shook his head. "No, sir. She didn't know I'm working here, and she didn't say anything to me after I told her. I hope she wasn't sad. I know she's been looking for work. Her family is still bad off."

Thad tapped his cheek, pretending to be confused. "Didn't the church send a wagonload of goods out to her house? She shouldn't be too terribly bad off after all that."

Jack snorted, bringing Thad to full attention. Why would he snort? Wasn't there enough in that wagonload of goods?

"That will get them by, and Kitty was so grateful, but food and clothes aren't the issue. It's the land. Her pa is gone. He hasn't been around in months. I don't know who he owed, but Kitty told me once that the house wasn't theirs. I don't know how much longer they can stay."

Katherine might be leaving? Warmth drained from his fingers. Here he'd been sitting, mulling over how to keep his feelings secret, thinking he'd done the family some great favor, when she was faced with losing her home. He'd been light with her about taking her skating, and she hadn't had the heart to tell him she wouldn't be there.

He couldn't let it stand.

"Thank you for telling me." Thad headed for the door.

"What are you going to do? There's no way you can buy a house from someone if you don't know who owns it."

Had he given himself away that boldly? "I don't think I mentioned buying their house."

Jack laughed. "Thad, you went out of your way to spend time alone with Kitty. That is, alone except for me. I'm young, not blind. But if you do care about her, you'll need to find out who owns that land. How will you do it?"

Thad knew her uncle owned the house and land after what her brothers had said while repairing the roof. If the loan was with Slade, in Damion's name, Slade was a good place to start. "Can you handle anyone who comes in?"

Jack laughed again. "No, but I'm good at acting like I can do anything. Just don't be gone long."

Thad grabbed his hat, stuffed it on his head, and pushed out the door into the street. Five years before, the entire main street had been macadamized to form a paved surface, leaving the roads without dust as they'd been before. The clear street also made seeing all the way to the end much easier than in the past.

Alex, Katherine's brother, was walking with his head down next to a man Thad had never seen in town before. He bore a striking resemblance to Alex's father; however, this man was well-dressed, walked tall, and weighed double what the missing man had weighed.

Thad waited until they were close enough for him to hear what the man was saying.

"Alex, go fetch some tobacco from the store. Tell him who to charge it to. I'm sure your father didn't have an account. I doubt they would've allowed it."

"He isn't going to give me any because he knows my pa never took credit, and he isn't going to just believe me when I say it's for someone else," Alex said.

The man reached out and smacked Alex on the back of the head, then grabbed his ear and hauled him toward the store.

"Excuse me." Thad stepped in his way. "I don't think we've met." Was this the owner of the house and land? If so, buying it and getting Katherine away from this man would be a top priority. Alex caught Thad's eye and silently pleaded for help.

"No, I don't think we have. Pardon me for just a moment while I teach this cur how to follow orders." He didn't wait for Thad to respond and instead shoved Alex into the store.

Thad followed, hanging back slightly. If he spoke too soon to save Alex right now, he might ruin his chances of buying the land without the man knowing there was more than just a desire to own land.

Cecil crossed his thick arms behind the counter and glared at the newcomer, but stayed silent.

"I sent this boy in here to fetch some tobacco for me. He refused to do it, saying you wouldn't give it to him. If I send my boy into the store, you will give him what he needs," the man said to Cecil.

"I will not," Cecil answered. "I might trust Alex, but I don't trust his pa, and you look a little too much like his pa for me to trust. You take yourself somewhere else to get tobacco. Maybe the Bullock store will serve you. I won't."

The man seethed, his chest quickly rising and falling. "How dare you say I'm not trustworthy. Do you have any idea who I am?"

"No." Cecil shook his head. "And if you were anyone around Deadwood, I would know or you'd have an account with me. You don't, so I'm not going to give you anything. I have no way of knowing if you'll pay me back. And I know Alex won't, because he's got no money. Take your hands off that boy. He told you the truth."

"Don't you dare tell me how to treat my property."

Cecil laughed, throwing his head back and cackling loud enough that it drew the attention of everyone in the bustling store. Alex was able to shake himself free of the hold on his ear with so much attention.

"I am Damion Horwath, owner of Leather and Fur Textiles Corporation, and you will never get my business now." He turned and headed for the door. "Alex, come. Now." He pointed to the spot next to him.

Alex trudged toward the door. The boy who'd been so excited to learn about roofing just a few days ago now looked hopeless. He didn't look up to see who was around, nor did he meet Thad's gaze. Thad followed them out into the street.

"Did you get your tobacco?" Thad asked, stopping Damion.

Damion turned. "I did not. It seems this town is even less cultured than I thought, but there are other stores."

Thad swallowed the bile in his throat. "Are you staying here? I run the mill and lumberyard in town, and I see most new faces before anyone else. Except perhaps the banker."

Damion adjusted his hat. Thad noted that though he'd just purchased new hats for all four boys, Alex wasn't wearing one.

"I did speak to the banker, but not about buying land. I already own the Horwath place, as run-down as it is. I will probably sell it next week after we move."

"We?" Thad hoped he wasn't pushing too hard for information, but men often liked talking about their plans.

"Yes, my brother appears to be deceased, which means I now have a family I didn't plan to have. His wife is pretty enough, and if she can't produce a son for me, there's always her daughter."

Thad again swallowed his revulsion. The man obviously thought no one would care about his sordid plans in a town as wild as Deadwood. Had Katherine come to tell Thad she wouldn't be staying, and he'd instead pushed his plans and hopes on her? How could she tell him what was happening? Then again, he'd never made his intentions fully clear. Even the kiss hadn't been discussed. Yet, he felt certain he shouldn't ask this man for her hand. That would give her uncle too much power.

"So, you're staying a week? Why is that? I can't imagine it's all that comfortable here if you're used to a large house."

"See, I knew you were a man who would understand. I'm being kind, generous if you will. I was asked to stay until the end of some shooting competition. Directly after, we'll be loading up and going home. I don't want to stay in Deadwood Gulch a moment longer than necessary. I may get a fair amount of fur from men around here, but I don't want to live here." He cringed. "Pardon me, I must be going. I only came to town for some tobacco, and it's taking much longer than I intended."

Thad touched his hat and stepped back to release him from their conversation. He had to get the truth from Katherine, but that wouldn't be easy with her uncle around. He doubted Damion would be as willing to let her speak to Thad as often or without restriction as Katherine's ma had, which would make finding out the truth difficult.

With hurried steps, Kitty ducked off the road back toward home. She usually kept to the road, but today something pressed her into the safety of the spruce trees. Her days in Deadwood were numbered, but she still couldn't bring herself to tell anyone about her family's situation. Who would believe her?

Through the trees, she heard the familiar sound of her uncle's brash voice and the mumble of her oldest brother. Alex was reaching an age where boys tested their father's patience, but he didn't have a father to test. Would he push Uncle Damion's boundaries, and if he did, what would Damion do?

The two passed quickly by her hiding spot and headed for Deadwood. A cool chill ran up her spine. If Thad had followed her, he would see Uncle Damion and would soon find out her situation. What would he do? He'd handled so much of what had gone wrong, but this wasn't something he could fix.

She craned her neck to see as far back toward town as possible, but both the town and her uncle were out of sight. Ma would know what to do. She would understand why Kitty couldn't tell Thad about how she'd entered the shooting contest. She would understand that Kitty couldn't shoot anyway. Ma would have ideas.

Kitty left the safety of the trees and rushed toward home. There was no telling how long Uncle Damion would be in town with Alex, but if he meant to rule the house with an iron heel on their throats, he wouldn't be gone long.

Ma sat outside with her knitting, her face pinched like it had been when they'd realized Pa wasn't coming home. "I saw Damion on the way to town," Kitty told her.

The yarn stalled for just a moment, then Ma whipped it around the needle and into the next stitch.

"He treats Alex like a dog. Worse than a dog." Ma squeezed the needles tightly.

"There has to be another way. A sure way. To make him leave. We can't take a chance that I'll miss. I haven't been able to practice outside of hunting for over a week." And not at all with the pink pistol except for when she'd shown it to Thad.

"If there is, I surely don't see it." Ma set her knitting aside and patted the bench next to her.

Kitty sat and waited for Ma to speak. She'd always been wise, the one the family went to with all their problems. "Kitty, we'll survive no matter what. You're a woman who has had to take on the burden of your father's position after he left. I know he trained you to shoot and to act like a man, but I don't think he ever meant for you to have to practice what he taught you."

"What if we just don't go? What if we refuse to get in his car when he decides to leave? Slavery isn't legal. He can't make us." Though Kitty couldn't imagine where else they would go. A family of six was a lot to care for; she knew from experience.

"He already told me if I try to fight him, he'll hold Daniel hostage until I go. I can't leave because he never goes anywhere without one of my boys with him. He doesn't care for their lives. He'd shoot any one of them without a care."

After seeing him with Alex, Kitty didn't doubt it. So, how were they going to live with him, and serve him, for seven years? Would any of them be alive by the end? "I can't shoot. The prize for the women's competition isn't enough to help, and if I compete against the men, like I signed up to do, I'll be shooting against Thad. He'll drop out and so will Amos. If they do, I win nothing because of the rules."

Ma swallowed hard and hung her head, then wove her fingers through Kitty's. "Then we'll have to pray for a way out or trust that God has a plan for us."

14

"Get that pie in the oven. It's getting late." Uncle Damion bustled into the kitchen, banging Ma's copper measuring cup against the table. "I will not have a late supper."

"Are you expecting someone?" Ma seemed to go even slower as she kneaded the dough for the crust.

Kitty slowed her pace in cutting the vegetables. If Ma could fight in her own way, Kitty would support her.

"And why would I invite anyone out here to this hovel?" Uncle Damion gestured to the roof. "My brother couldn't take care of the grass, much less the house I let him live in. This won't sell for half what it would've made if he would've tried to care for it."

"You could let us fix it, then sell later." Kitty didn't look up, afraid he would sense her hope and take it away, even though he would be the one to gain.

"And just how would you pay for the repairs? Do

you have some money hidden away? I doubt it. If you had, you would've paid me to keep me away. Don't think I don't know how you talk about me behind my back."

"And why wouldn't we? You're being a tyrant." Ma grabbed the rolling pin and leveled it over the dough but did not start rolling.

Uncle Damion moved much faster than Kitty had expected with his large frame, and he yanked the rolling pin from Ma's hand and raised it to strike her.

"Don't you dare!" Kitty shoved Ma out of the way and stood tall, waiting for the blow.

"Don't you ever get in the way of my discipline, or you'll get it double," he growled.

Kitty didn't figure he could do anything more than Pa already had. "Don't threaten Ma."

He gripped her arm and tugged her away from Ma. "What did you say to me?"

A knock sounded on the door, and Damion released her and turned to answer it. He tugged the door open, and Thad waited on the other side. Kitty rubbed her arm and hoped Thad hadn't heard the raised voices. The wood of the walls and doors was thin.

"Good afternoon." Thad took off his hat though he hadn't been invited inside yet.

"What are you doing here? Are you following me?" Damion accused.

Kitty wanted to gasp but held it tightly inside. Had Thad spoken to Uncle Damion? Did he know about what was happening? She quickly gathered all the root vegetables and the chopped onion and put them into the soup pot to soften.

"Actually, I came to see Katherine. She was helping me set up the targets for the shooting competition, and I'd hoped to ask her a few questions." He leaned to the side and caught her eye.

Warmth spread over her, and she bit her lip. They had finished setting up the targets, so Thad had to have something else he wanted to say. He must have been aware of Uncle Damion's plans to take them, or he would've spoken plainly. Kitty set down her spoon and took off her apron.

"Just where do you think you're going?" Damion moved in front of her. "You can't just leave when there's supper to prepare."

"Perhaps we should invite our guest to eat with us?" Ma moved back to her place and quickly rolled the dough flat.

"I can't stay, but thank you." Thad smiled Ma's way. "May I speak to Katherine? We can talk on the driveway, never leaving the front yard."

Kitty waited, wanting to go, but knew the more she looked like she wanted something, the less likely she was to get it. "I'll only be a few minutes. I have to wait for those to boil for at least fifteen minutes before I can make the gravy." Though Ma always made better gravy anyway.

"Daniel!" Uncle Damion yelled. "Get in here."

Daniel ran in from the backyard carrying a slingshot and three large granite stones. "I'm here."

"Follow these two." He pointed at Kitty. "It's

promiscuous to go walking around with a man. You'll take Daniel with you. Daniel, you are not to leave Kitty. Do you understand me?"

Daniel furrowed his brow. "I've never had to go with her before, and Mr. Easton has been here plenty of times. He even helped us fix the roof. If it weren't for him, you'd have rain on your head tonight when that storm comes in." Daniel laughed.

Uncle Damion's face flushed a deep crimson, and he gripped Daniel's ear, forcing him to look Damion in the eye. "You will stay by her side. Do you understand me?"

Daniel was still young, and tears glistened in his eyes. Kitty wanted to slap her uncle's hand away, but she didn't dare. Not if she wanted to find out what Thad had to say.

"Is that really necessary?" Thad crossed his arms.

"Apparently it is, since the boy won't listen." He released Daniel with a shove. "Be back before you're needed."

Ma turned slightly and caught Kitty's eye, letting her know that she would get the supper done if Kitty wasn't back the moment the vegetables were ready. She gave Ma a nod of understanding, then followed Thad outside. Her heart raced until she felt light-headed.

What could he possibly know, and how would he talk to her with Daniel plastered to her side?

If Katherine's uncle had no fear of treating his family so poorly in front of a stranger—one who could be argued to have power within the town—then he would be much worse in secret. Thad couldn't let him take the Horwath family from their home. He'd have to find a way to gain their freedom.

Katherine followed him down the lane, but still within view of the house. He stopped and waited for Daniel to join them. If a little spy was what Damion wanted, that's what he would get. But he wouldn't get all he hoped for because, after helping the family with the roof, Thad had Daniel's loyalty, which meant much more than blood relation.

"Miss Horwath, you seem tense today."

Her glance skittered back to the house. "I shouldn't leave Ma alone with him for too long. Uncle Damion is uncouth and too large for Ma's safety."

Katherine's veiled words seized his stomach. "Then I'll be fast. I'm concerned." Little Daniel's ears perked up, just as Thad had hoped they would.

"About what?" Katherine turned to fully face him. He hated the lines marring her forehead with fear for her mother.

"There's talk in town that the shooter no one knows is a cover for someone else."

Katherine's face drained of color, and he braced himself to catch her if she fell. He'd suspected that name was hers, but wasn't sure how he'd deal with the situation. Now he was in a bind. She needed the prize money more than anyone else. Yet if he shot against her, he'd lose his standing in the community, which would hurt the whole town. Not to mention take away his ability to help her and care for her family after they got rid of her uncle.

It wasn't like the prize money would solve every problem. Once the house payments were made for a few months with the winnings, the family still needed to eat and have clothing. And their needs wouldn't stop as soon as their uncle went back where he came from.

Thad needed his standing within the community to keep Jack working, to keep his house, and to help the Horwaths. But if he dropped out of the contest, Katherine would lose by forfeit. Amos most certainly wouldn't shoot against a woman.

"Daniel, I need you to go find one of those pink rocks Ma likes so much. There's a pile of stones just over there." Katherine pointed a few yards away. "You know the pile. You'll be close enough to hear us."

"If Damion gets angry with me…"

"I'll take the blame." If it were possible, Katherine paled more.

The moment the boy rushed off, Thad dropped all pretense of talking about the contest. There was no time. "Katherine, I'm not worried about the competition. We'll let it handle itself. I'm concerned for you. Marry me. Let me get you out of this situation right now, and we'll work together to free your family."

Her mouth dropped open, and her eyes widened. "Marry you? I can't do that. Thad… You'll lose all credibility if you marry me. My father set us on this course, and I aim to fix it. Somehow."

"You…don't want to marry me?" He'd never considered, though the idea had come in a flash, that she would refuse.

"Thad, you hardly know me. I can't leave my mother for more than a few minutes. How could I leave her and marry? Not to mention my uncle would never allow it right now." A hint of color returned to her cheeks along with a hint of a smile. "Though I did enjoy when we pretended to be wed a few days ago."

He reached for her hand, then thought better of it. If her uncle saw any outward affection from him, that would make this task all the harder. "I wasn't pretending, Katherine. I don't think you were, either."

She ducked her head to hide a full smile. "No, I certainly was not."

"Do you trust me?" Thad ached to hear at least that. Maybe she didn't love him now—since a feeling so deep couldn't be expected yet—but he could do what needed to be done if she could only trust him.

"I can. I do." She glanced back to the house. "What do you need from me?"

"I know your uncle plans to take you away. I need you to trust me that I won't let that happen. I want you to know that I'm a man of my word and that I can take care of you and your family. I don't know how to get you free of this threat right now, but I won't stop until he's gone."

Katherine slowly nodded. "If you're asking me to trust you, then I must be honest with you. You may not want to help me after what I've done."

Thad waited, wanting very much to show her he wasn't at her side only for times of good.

"I asked Jack to sign up for the shooting competition under a false name. The other man who no one knows...is me. I needed the money for my family. I'd hoped to win it before my uncle came so we could send the money as if my father had been the one to send it as usual. I'm sorry for tricking you."

Her honesty touched him. "Daniel," Thad called to the boy a few feet away. When he didn't answer, Thad knew the boy hadn't been listening. "Daniel!" he called a little louder, though he didn't want to alert Damion to Daniel's lack of attention.

"Yes, sir?" The boy poked his head up from the rock pile.

"Give your sister one of those flowers there by the pile, please."

Daniel shot to his feet, brushed off his knees and picked a pretty white wildflower, then gave it to Katherine. "There you go." He smiled up at her. "I think I found a rock for Ma."

"Go and get it, we'll wait." Thad waited until Daniel was a few steps away before finishing his thought. "I understand your motives, and they were pure. If I had my way, women wouldn't be excluded from the competition. At the very least, they'd have their own with an equal prize."

Daniel gathered the rock and headed back toward them, chucking it between his hands.

"I'll go, but we'll talk soon," Thad said.

She gave him a weak smile. "I trust you."

15

The only way to prevent Damion from forcing his family into labor was to pay for the house. Thad considered how he could make an offer on the house without involving the man who owned it. If the loan was originally through the bank, he could pay it and then Katherine and her family would be free. That is, if anyone contested Damion's right to take them. He could argue he was merely looking out for his family. Thad knew the truth, but would anyone care who had any sort of power to make him stop?

Therein lay the trouble. The Horwath family was not only poor, but the patriarch of the family had made a nuisance of himself for years. Many people breathed a sigh of relief when he would leave town on one of his hunting expeditions. The fact that he hadn't come home was something to be celebrated.

Thad headed for the bank, hopeful Mr. Slade

would be able to give him either information or a way to solve this issue without further involving Damion Horwath. He stopped by the desk of Mr. Slade's assistant and waited to be noticed.

"May I help you?" the assistant asked without looking up.

"Is Mr. Slade available for a consultation?"

The man set his pencil down on the huge ledger he'd been writing in. "I'll go see if he's free. One moment."

Thad compared his own experience to the one Jack had told him about. Granted, Jack was still young and had been even younger then. It was possible Mr. Slade had been concerned the boy had no intention of ever using an account. That didn't make up for the issue of stealing from him though.

The door opened, and Mr. Slade's assistant came back out, then silently sat in his chair. "He'll be out shortly. Please have a seat." He indicated the two wooden chairs outside Slade's office. They looked like they were meant to make a man uncomfortable in every way possible.

Thad ambled to the seats, hoping if he took his time Slade would appear before he had to wait. He lowered into the chair and watched everyone work around him. He hadn't taken a day off of work in so long that he felt lazy sitting there.

Mr. Slade's door opened slightly. "Easton, come on in." He opened the door slightly wider. "What brings you to my office?"

Thad waited until Mr. Slade had the door closed

and had taken a few steps away from it before he answered. He lowered into the leather-covered chair in front of Mr. Slade's huge desk. "I'm wondering who owns the Horwath place. I know they are in a bind, and I might like to help them."

Mr. Slade laughed slightly. "No sense in getting your hands dirty. They have family here now to help them. I don't have the loan, and I believe Aspen's brother owns the place outright."

Which left Thad no recourse, unless he guessed the amount Aspen owed to live there, took out a loan, and offered to pay the uncle to leave. But would he leave? He seemed to enjoy the fact that his brother had disappeared, leaving him with six people to serve him.

"I heard the deputy over in Belle Fourche was a Pinkerton once," Thad mused. Maybe what he needed was someone to go find Aspen. If the brother was found, Damion would have no legal standing. He could make them leave their home, but he couldn't force them to work to pay off the debt.

"He was. A few years ago, anyway. I don't know much about him other than that he refuses to ride a horse. I don't mind. Since he drives, he makes it a point to visit nearby towns. His wife is rather social as well." Slade clasped his hands in front of him.

Thad only cared if the man would be willing to look into someone who'd gone missing. The Deadwood sheriff was too busy doing his duty here to take the time to leave and look for a man who'd gone off all on his own. A trip to see Blake Longfellow might actually solve two of Thad's problems if he asked the right questions.

"Thank you. That's all I needed to know."

"If you want the land, I would think it would be available shortly. Damion Horwath came in here to talk yesterday. He told me he didn't want to be tied to that property anymore. Once it sells, he won't be obligated to come back. I don't know where the family will go, but they don't own the land or house, so they can be made to leave at any point." He opened a desk drawer and pulled out a tablet of paper. "By the way, how are the sales and entry numbers looking for the shooting contest? I'd meant to ask you when I was helping at the range last week, but Nancy is quite the distraction." Mr. Slade laughed a little too loudly.

"Yes, a distraction." Of the worst kind, Thad thought. "We'll have just enough to pay the winner and pay for the lumber and supplies to build the rink. Nothing else. Unless we have a much larger turnout than the last few years."

"Which is possible. If that deputy's wife comes from Belle Fourche, perhaps some of her friends will come to watch. Word could spread. Did you put up any posters in Lead?"

Thad had put up posters everywhere he'd been allowed to. "Yes, and I also got pledges from Cecil and Grainger over at the blacksmith shop. They are donating even more than usual because they know the need is great." He loved putting the competition together, but gathering pledges and keeping track of the tickets was his least favorite part.

"I'm going to be honest with you. I know you think Kitty Horwath is a big draw, but I think you're mistaken. That family is trouble. She hasn't signed up yet, and I couldn't be happier. If she signs up, people will think she'll win without trying. It's better this way."

Thad slid his hat back on his head and stood. "I guess we'll have to agree to disagree. Thank you for your help and the information." He let himself out before Mr. Slade could ask anything further.

THAD SELDOM HAD reason to leave Deadwood, so he rarely used his horse, much less a car. Thankfully, his friend who worked for the local newspaper wasn't using his automobile that afternoon, allowing Thad to make the twenty-eight mile drive to Belle Fourche in a little over an hour. By horse the route would've taken much longer, and Thad had already lost most of the day.

He reached the sheriff's office late in the afternoon, and when he went inside, he saw a young man sitting behind a desk thumbing through a stack of Wanted posters. The man glanced up, and only then did Thad notice the smattering of gray in his hair. "Are you Blake Longfellow?"

The man laid down the posters. "I am. What can I do for you?"

After a day of worry, a slight relief pulled Thad's

shoulders up. "I'm hoping you can help me, perhaps in more ways than one."

"I'm listening." Blake folded his hands in front of him.

Thad explained how Aspen Horwath had gone missing a few months before and that his brother was now posing a threat to Aspen's family. "I'm hoping I can hire you to look for Aspen. If we find him, then hopefully his brother will go home."

"I don't go hunting for people anymore. That isn't my job. I know a few people who might be willing to help, but, I'm sorry, that's not part of my job anymore."

Thad couldn't blame the man. Especially with the places Aspen Horwath often went. He bragged about how dangerous the situations were.

"Is this a situation where you think this man could be found? I got the impression everyone believes him to be dead," Blake asked.

"His family believes he isn't coming home. I need to make sure of that fact."

"I see." Blake drummed his fingers on the desk. "I have a friend, Mac, who might be looking for a job. If you have any idea where the man was headed, that will help in looking for him more quickly. I'm assuming time is of the essence?"

"Yes, he was headed to the Badlands, and the family is leaving in six days." Right after the shooting competition. Sooner if Damion got wind something might get in the way of his plan.

"Why don't you come with me, and we'll go out to talk to Mac. What was the other thing you wanted me to do for you?"

Thad snorted slightly. "Honestly, this would be something your wife could do for me. She's friends with Katherine Horwath."

"Yes, Kitty. We've met. I wondered if that was the same Horwath family you meant."

Thad gave a quick nod. "It is. Your wife is signed up for the shooting competition, as is Katherine, but under a man's name in the elite division."

"Oh, that's passing strange. I wonder why she did that," Blake said.

"To win the prize money she needs for her family. If the two men who are registered drop out of the running because they don't want to shoot against a woman, Katherine will lose by default."

"So you want Hannah to enter the elite competition under a man's name so that if the two men drop out, Kitty will still have someone to compete against and could possibly win?"

"Yes, that was my plan exactly. And if she loses, at least it's not because she wasn't given the chance to try."

Blake grinned. "I like you and the way you think. I'll let Hannah know, and I'm sure she'll want to enter right away."

"You may want to enter for her. The signup is in the pawnshop, and the owner might question a woman signing up."

Blake gathered his hat and adjusted it on his brow.

"I'll do that. Let me go tell the sheriff I'll be out for a little while, then you can ride with me and tell Mac what you need. If all goes well, you can be back on the road to Deadwood before the supper hour."

Thad certainly hoped so. The car wasn't his, and he didn't want to have it out after dark. At least the days were getting longer and the temperature was staying warmer later.

Thad rode with Blake out to a ranch about a half hour outside of Belle Fourche. The wooden arch at the end of the driveway said "Johlman." As Blake pulled to a stop, a woman who looked to be in her fifties came out to see him. "Blake, who have you brought with you?"

Blake grinned. "Someone for Mac to meet. Is he available?"

The woman made a show of rolling her eyes. "You know him, stubborn as a mule. I tried to tell him it was too early to be digging in the garden, but that's what he's doing."

Blake leaned toward Thad. "That's my sister. She isn't related to the Johlmans, but Mrs. Johlman was injured a few years back, and having my sister here helps them. Mac works the ranch along with Gideon and Leo Johlman."

Too many names for him to keep track of. "I'm only concerned with Mac," Thad said.

"Follow me." Blake led the way to a lush green backyard. There, a man had made a sizeable dent in the plot that needed digging.

"Mac. I've got a job for you. If you're up for it."

Mac laughed before he turned around. "You know me, Blake. I'm always up for an adventure."

16

The rifle sat waiting by the back door, but Kitty didn't want to leave to go hunting. Not until Uncle Damion headed into town. Ma had been tired again, now that Damion was here, and Kitty worried for her health. She didn't want to leave Ma alone in the house with him.

"You'd best get going soon. If there isn't something simmering on the stove in the next hour, he'll come in here and start throwing things around."

"I can't leave you here alone." Kitty cut a glance toward the small sitting room and the haze of tobacco smoke slowly filling the house. "We could plan a meal with no meat. This wouldn't be the first time." Nor the last unless Thad could come up with a plan.

The flower Thad had given her the day before still lay on the windowsill. She knew he'd had her brother gather it only so Damion didn't see Thad's actions and realize what was happening.

"He won't agree," Ma said. "Perhaps your father still has some traps set along his old line? Are they worth checking?"

Kitty shook her head. "I took all of them in shortly after he left because I don't like them. Half the time the animals are wounded, and then I have to shoot an animal that's been suffering. I'd rather just take a clean shot and be done with it."

Ma laid a hand on her shoulder. "Considering your father taught you all about hunting and shooting, you certainly have different ideas, and I'm thankful for that."

Part of Kitty's feelings came from church. Pa had never gone and thought churchgoing was a waste of a perfectly good Sunday. He'd never made his children be quiet or respect the Sabbath. In fact, he'd usually put them to work doing something he didn't want to do himself. It wasn't until Kitty was an adult that she tried to keep the Sabbath as a day of rest.

She was heading for the back door when she heard a soft *plink* against the front window like a pebble hitting the glass. Ma went to see who'd done it and snorted as she opened the door to Thad.

"Mrs. Horwath, are you alone?" he whispered.

"Never. Let's follow Kitty out back. The windows are still swollen shut on that side of the house, and we can speak without being heard." She shuffled him down the hall and right into Kitty.

"Sorry." Thad kept his voice low, then grinned slightly as he opened the door for her, almost putting his arm around her in the process.

Kitty was certain she didn't want to go hunting now. "What's wrong?" she asked.

He motioned for her to keep going farther from the house before he would speak. When they reached the trees, Ma sat on a fallen log. "I think we're far enough away to speak as long as we watch the house and listen for anyone coming."

Kitty kneeled on the ground and lay the rifle across her lap. "What's wrong, Thad?" She hadn't realized she'd called him by his given name in front of Ma until she noticed the silence and glanced in Ma's direction.

"We'll talk later," Ma said before nodding to Thad to let him speak.

"I spoke to Mr. Slade. I know he's not the only banker in town, but he does the most lending as far as homes and land. He didn't lend Damion the money for this property, though they are friends."

"People with similar bank accounts often are." Ma frowned.

Kitty wanted to defend Thad. He'd helped them in so many ways, but Ma didn't know that. She thought the church had sent out all the food and goods. She thought Thad had only been getting rid of old shingles when he'd given them for their roof. She also thought Thad had charged Kitty for the pistol since she'd said she wanted to pay him back, when he'd actually never asked for anything.

"Not everyone, I promise you." Thad smiled, unaffected by Ma's statement. "But that leads to a problem. I was going to offer to buy the house, then you could pay me back as you were able to—if you were able to. I wasn't concerned about that part. I only want to get you free of this situation. But Mr. Slade wasn't helpful."

"That's not surprising," Ma said. "I can't help you with the loan information. I'm not certain any bank was used. This land originally belonged to Aspen and Damion's parents and was a very nice property. Aspen inherited the house, and Damion inherited the money. When Aspen had some trouble after the last Deadwood fire, Damion helped, but what he really wanted was the house and land. So, Aspen gave Damion the house and is now forced to pay in order to stay in it."

Kitty had never heard that. She'd only known that they'd come to Deadwood when Ma was pregnant with her, and they'd raised all five children there in the old house.

"So the house is deeded to Damion, and he's only letting you rent it. That will make this situation even more difficult. I really think when you come to town for Sunday service, someone needs to take you in so you don't ever have to leave with this man."

"Do you think the town will bother?" Ma snorted. "We've lived out here for twenty years and no one—until recently—has cared if we were hungry, or cold, or needy. There have been times I didn't even have wool yarn to knit socks. It's mighty easy to avoid the poor and pray for them than it is to help."

Kitty could stay silent no longer. "Ma, he knows. He's helped. He's the one who sent all the food."

Thad shook his head. "Who sent help doesn't

matter because really the help came too late. We need to focus on what we can do now."

The loud crack of a pistol cocking silenced all three of them.

"I think you've worn out your welcome, Mr. Easton."

Thad was glad for the pistol he'd strapped to his side before coming out to see the Horwaths. Normally he didn't bother. While Deadwood was a rough town, during the broad light of day it was much like any other town he'd live in. Only in certain areas and after dark did one need to be concerned. Except when one was going somewhere to upset the apple cart, like he was doing with Damion Horwath.

"Why don't you head back where you belong." Damion waved the barrel of the pistol from the center of Thad's chest toward the direction of the driveway. "And if you think for one minute you're going to try to trick me, think again. You go right ahead and get all the money you think you'll need to pay me for this house. I'll take it and still take my family with me. If you try to stop me, I'll have you arrested. If you think you'll take them away before that infernal shooting competition, I'll take them before that."

Thad wasn't sure why Damion had agreed to stay until then, but he wasn't going to question it. Then again, even if Katherine won now, she couldn't pay the debt. Damion would never consider it paid in full, and he'd take them away anyway. There was no solution besides force.

"It might interest you to know that I've hired a man to look for Aspen," Thad said.

Damion aimed the pistol at Thad again. "You won't find him. He's long gone. Traders got him."

"How do you know?" Ma asked, deathly quiet. "You said you hadn't heard from him in over two months, which was why you came. We didn't even know where he'd gone. How did you?"

"I have my ways. And let's not forget that he was gone for two months. You knew about our payment arrangement, but you didn't send me a message to let me know about the missing payment or that my brother was missing. Obviously, you need someone to look after you. You're not capable of looking after yourself."

Thad inched to the side, away from Katherine and her ma. If anyone were accidentally shot in this situation, it would be him. He didn't want to see anyone get hurt, but Katherine and her mother the least.

Damion followed Thad step-by-step until they were halfway down the driveway and too far for Katherine or her mother to hear. Damion carefully released the cocking hammer on the pistol. "If you come to this house again, I'll shoot you. If you so much as try to talk to Kitty anywhere, I'll take them right then. I'm only staying because I feel like watching Kitty compete. I want to know just how good she is at shooting before I take her under my roof."

Thad got the sickening suspicion that if Damion feared her, he'd accuse her of murdering her father and she would have no way to hire a lawyer. If he never returned, he was as good as dead. "Let me take her. Then you don't have to worry." Thad was pleading with the enemy, but if it would get him what he wanted, then plead he would.

Damion snorted. "And then what? Do you think Kitty would stop until she got her family back? You seem to be a man of means, and she'll spend every penny you have to your name in lawyers and anything else to make me do what I will not do." He took a step closer and lowered his voice to a whisper. "What you don't know, and what Kitty doesn't know either, is that Aspen had a will. I know because I drew it up."

Thad forced his knees to hold him upright. They wanted to buckle. "How did Aspen Horwath have a will?"

Damion snorted. "He didn't want one. He was sure he didn't need one. The man was far too sure of himself. I convinced him that if he was planning to go confront the men he wanted to, he should have a failsafe for his family. That failsafe was me. He left me as the guardians of his wife and children. So, you see, Mr. Easton, the law is on my side. Now get off my property."

Kitty ran headlong into the woods, fear and anger pushing her farther than she usually allowed herself to go. The louder she was, the less likely she'd shoot anything for supper, but that detail didn't matter.

She tripped over a loose stone and stumbled to her knees, her rifle sliding a few feet away and landing at the foot of a spindly tree. Tears burned her eyes, but she wouldn't let them fall. One by one, every opportunity for escape was blocked. All that was left was the competition, and she had the sinking suspicion that Damion wouldn't be placated by money now.

Seven years. She'd be almost thirty by then. Thad would probably marry someone else. While men often waited until age twenty-five to marry, women didn't. Maybe she should've taken Thad's hurried proposal when she'd had the chance.

"Kitty?" Alex's voice traveled through the trees. "Don't shoot. Where are you?"

If there had ever been any chance she was going to shoot something for supper before, there was none now. "I'm here." She rose off her knees and turned over to sit on a flat rock.

Alex sat at her side and sighed. "You know how I have always had that tree in the front yard where I sit and hide from Ma and Pa?"

She nodded, not sure what he wanted to say, though he was too old for tree houses now.

"I was sitting up there hiding when Uncle Damion chased Thad off the property with his gun, but it's what he said that was the most interesting. I think he killed Pa. I think he did it on purpose, and I think he tricked him into writing a will to make what he's doing legal."

"Then there is no fighting it?" She'd wanted to believe Thad, that he could help. He'd asked her to trust him, and she had, but if there were nothing he could do…

"He told Thad that if he tried to go near you, he'd take us away before the shooting competition. I don't know what we're going to do, but we'll have to do it without his help."

Kitty laid a hand on Alex's arm that she hoped was calming for him, though it certainly wasn't for her. Not with the thoughts bouncing around in her head. "I promise you, I'll go to prison before I let him take any of us, and I'm a mighty crack shot."

17

The meeting the day before with Mr. Slade had rankled Thad into action. Not only did he want to make sure Hannah would get signed up under the elite competition, he wanted to pay to have Katherine signed up for the women's division, just so people would stop thinking the mysterious name was hers—no matter that it was.

If no one worried, the competitors wouldn't drop out. In fact, if they were curious, Katherine's being signed up might cause more people to come. If that were the case, Thad would petition Mr. Slade again for a bigger prize for the women.

Thad tugged open the pawnshop door and marched right to the front, ignoring whomever else might be there. The sooner he finished his business, the better. He still needed to find a foolproof way of helping Katherine, and there were few days left to make it happen.

"Dalton, do you have the signup sheet?" he called to the proprietor, who was helping a young man pick out silver coins.

"It's right where you left it." Dalton nodded toward the tattered paper on the other end of the counter. The sheet had been there for over a month and had obviously been handled by many people. Thad scanned the list and mentally tallied the dollars he'd have to collect from Dalton, though the man had insisted on keeping one percent of each entry for his trouble.

Thad stood to the side, waiting for Dalton to finish so he could sign Katherine up for the women's competition. A heavy floral scent accosted his nose, one he immediately recognized as belonging to Nancy Powers.

"Why, Mr. Easton! How nice to see you out of your office. Isn't it lovely that we have so many people interested in our little contest?" She fluttered her lashes at him.

He didn't miss that she'd called it *theirs* when she'd had little to nothing to do with it besides wasting his time and signing up to participate. "There are quite a few names, yes."

Mr. Slade walked in and tipped his hat to someone in the back, caught Thad's eye, then headed right for him. Thad couldn't make his distaste known, but these were the exact people he'd hoped to avoid.

"Thad, good to see you checking on matters. I was just in to do that very thing." He reached for the list and lowered his spectacles on his nose. "Very interesting."

"Isn't it?" Nancy laughed. "I think it's wonderful that Kitty Horwath isn't shooting this year. I know for a fact a lot of women said they weren't going to compete if she signed up. I told them they'd have no problem winning against her as long as the targets don't look like squirrels."

Mr. Slade laughed along with Nancy.

"I don't think Miss Horwath will have any trouble shooting the targets," Thad said. He tried to catch Dalton's attention, but Dalton had moved on to an elderly woman who was haggling with him over the price of wire egg baskets.

An uneasiness washed over Thad—a sense of foreboding he couldn't name—like an attack was on the horizon.

Mr. Slade arched an eyebrow. "You know, Thad here has been mighty interested in helping the Horwath family. We should sweeten the deal for the winner a little bit."

Thad looked between the two people and stiffened his spine. He hadn't meant to make himself so plain. Doing so only put both him and Katherine in danger of scorn in the public eye.

"What do you have in mind?" Nancy smiled, leaning forward like they shared a devious secret.

"You seem interested in Thad as much as he's interested in helping the Horwaths. Why don't we make the prize even sweeter for the town? Whoever wins the women's shooting competition will go to luncheon with Thad. Goodness knows he's the most eligible man in town."

Nancy clapped her hands together quickly. "I love it, and should it lead to more outings, I wouldn't complain, either." Her gaze fell on Thad with more longing than an untrained dog for a piece of meat.

Thad took a step back. "And what if the deputy's wife should win? What good is that prize to her?" He hoped he sounded sensible. He hadn't planned to have to defend himself in the middle of the pawnbroker's shop that morning.

"If she wins, I'll pay for her and her husband." Mr. Slade brushed off his concern. "But the only way this will make any difference is if Kitty is signed up. A rivalry between two women will draw a crowd." He snapped his fingers to get Dalton's attention.

The older pawnbroker gave the man a side-eye that would've knocked a lesser—or wiser—man off his feet. "I'll be with you when I'm finished here."

"I don't like the idea of Kitty competing. The whole reason I was excited was because she always wins." Nancy fluffed her bottom lip out in a full pout. "The others will drop out if she enters."

"If you want time with the man, you'll just have to be better than Kitty. I'm sure you can manage." Mr. Slade laughed and waved the broker over.

"What can I do for you?" Dalton growled, then spit a wad of tobacco in the corner.

Nancy shuddered and turned away. Thad couldn't blame her. He'd never been interested in starting the habit, but seeing it in action made the temptation even less.

"We need to sign Kitty Horwath up for the women's competition." Mr. Slade pulled out his thick money clip and slapped a paper dollar on the counter.

Of course the man would pay in paper, the kind of money that was frivolous in the West. If he hadn't been heavily protected by his associations, he wouldn't survive in wild Deadwood.

"Kitty?" Dalton glanced between all three of them. "Why ain't she in here paying her own dues?"

Thad stepped back and let Mr. Slade handle the explanation. If he wanted to pay her entry fee, that meant Thad didn't have to say anything. He'd keep his association secret a little longer, keeping prying eyes off Katherine.

"Because she's too poor to do it herself, and we need her in the competition to bring in a crowd. Especially if she and Nancy here are in a battle for love."

"Wait just one minute." Thad found his voice. "No one said anything about love. You said one visit to the café. That's it. I didn't even agree to that much."

Nancy clung to his arm. "You wouldn't make a fool of me. I know you wouldn't. My father would make you pay if you did," she hissed under her breath.

Her father was the man who'd started clearing lumber from around the town and delivering it to the lumberyard to be sold. He'd started with deadfall, then had thinned out treed areas that were too thick and a risk of fire, then had moved to other areas of the

Black Hills. Nancy's father wasn't one Thad could risk angering since the lumber he sold largely came from him.

"I wouldn't shame you, but you shouldn't put yourself in this position," Thad said. He hated confrontational women, much preferring those who asked for what they desired directly and took an answer as an answer. Pestering bothered him more than he could stand.

"The only one who appears uncomfortable with it is you," she muttered, smiling at Mr. Slade. "I'm sure I can manage to best her. I have in every other way." Her pointed gaze swung back to Thad as if he were yet another thing she'd accomplished.

"Good! Good, indeed. I'll go to the newspaper and ask them to print up some posters. Rush delivery!" Mr. Slade said. "Nancy, you'll go all over town and have them put up."

She gasped, sputtering. "What?"

"Well, I certainly can't. I've got work to do at the bank."

Nancy stared at Thad, expecting him to immediately come to her rescue. He wouldn't, as he too had to get back to work, and her attitude left much to be desired.

"Fine. I'll hire Jack to do it. He's always loitering about, looking for work." Her nose inched higher in the air.

Dalton scribbled Kitty's name down on the form and stuck the dollar in the till. "Is there anything else you need from me? You picked a busy day to gather in the worst possible place." He tapped the counter. "Maybe move along."

Thad wished, in some respects, he had the same freedom as the old pawnbroker to be who he was and let the others in town think what they would. But he couldn't. His business hinged on pleasing those wealthy people in town. They were the ones building new stores and homes. He was sure not to offend or hurt those who weren't in those positions, as they needed houses and barns as well, but those people rarely came to see him twice.

Thad left the building before Nancy could follow him. Since he didn't want her to hire Jack to do work for her and potentially treat him poorly, he'd send Jack out to Katherine's house to let her know she would be shooting in the women's competition. He couldn't go out there himself and risk being seen.

"Thad!" Nancy called from behind him.

People in the street eyed him like vultures, waiting to see how he'd respond. He stopped and turned, plastering a smile on his face. "Yes?"

She hurried toward him with tiny steps and reached for his hand to help her step onto the walkway. Her hand slipped through his, then wouldn't let go. "Walk with me."

He took a deep breath and stayed at her side, but tried to tuck her hand to his arm. Courteous, but not intimate. She refused and gripped his hand tighter. He refused to cause a scene over something so small. "All right, I'm walking."

"Mr. Slade has already gone over to have the

posters printed. I wanted you to know that I will do whatever it takes to win this competition. I think you and I have an exceedingly bright future together. With my father's abundance of lumber and your ability to sell it, we'd be fools not to consider a...partnership."

The way she'd said "partnership" made his spine tense. If he'd found Nancy more pleasant, and perhaps if he'd found Katherine less so, he might have been willing to entertain the notion of a marriage of convenience to Nancy. Especially as it would stop all the well-meaning, but patently annoying older ladies at the church from trying to marry him off.

Unfortunately, none of those things were the case. He had to be kind to Nancy because she was right—her father provided a huge portion of the lumber he sold. Thad telling Mr. Powers that he wasn't interested in his daughter might be even worse than telling his daughter he wanted no partnership with her.

"I didn't realize you had such an interest in your father's business dealings."

She laughed softly. "I don't. Except when it suits me." She glanced up and down the street. "I'm going to have to find that boy. I won't be walking door-to-door with posters. I have better things to do with my time than manual labor." She gave him a fierce smile. "Like practice my aim."

"I'm sure there are young men or women who would be willing to do the job for you. Honest work is welcome. In fact, I must get back to mine." He gently pried his hand from her hold.

"I'll let my father know about our future dealings. He'll be pleased to know you agree."

Thad gritted his teeth. Was he going to have to draw a line in the sand for this woman? "I haven't agreed to any partnership yet. Good day, Miss Powers." He touched his hat and crossed the street a little earlier than necessary to head for the lumberyard. What in the world was he going to do about Nancy, especially if her father planned a marriage between them?

18

Ma glanced out the window, then pushed a glass of lemonade toward Kitty. "Drink. You look like you haven't stopped for a drink in two days."

Kitty felt like she hadn't. She'd told Damion she was going hunting so she could get out of the house, since that was the one time he allowed her out of his sights without one of her brothers along. But what she'd seen in town had her running all the way back home. And she didn't even have any meat to show for her trouble.

"He was with Nancy." She didn't even feel empty enough to cry. Thad had kissed Kitty and helped her family. He'd made her promise to trust him, and she'd let her heart believe he wasn't like any of the other wealthy men who took advantage of the poor.

But he'd been holding hands with Nancy. There was no two ways about it. He'd held her hand. He'd smiled at her. He'd walked her down the street, holding her closely tucked against his side—a place Kitty had wanted to be...until now.

Oh, who was she kidding, the only reason she was so out of sorts was because Nancy had again made a fool of her.

"Nancy likes to push people." Ma sighed heavily. "I know you're out of sorts because of what Damion said. But I think you know that if you are meant to be with Thad, Damion is not going to stop you."

"What about Thad? Will he stop me?" Kitty clenched her jaw tightly. "He was the one reaching out to her. He knows I don't go into town that often and wouldn't see him. I guess now I know why he was so willing to walk around with her all day while Jack and I worked to set up the shooting contest. He likes her company."

But why had he gone out of his way to help her family and come see her? Why had he offered to help as if he were interested? What could his reason possibly be? Unless he, like others, simply wanted to give her family a lesson after the things her father had done. She couldn't recall her father ever having cheated the lumberyard, but perhaps he had.

"There's always more than one side to a story, Kitty. You know that. Everyone thinks your pa was just a wily coyote of a man who took advantage of everyone. He wasn't always that way, but having kindness repaid with scorn will do that. It got so bad that he started plotting against people, assuming they'd treat him badly no matter what he did anyway."

Kitty had never known Pa as a kind man, only one who taught her to be the best she could be, just in case she had to be. All that training finally made sense. Maybe he had cared for her in his own way. He'd set her up to be able to defend herself and her family in his absence.

"Well, I have no way of verifying Thad's side of the story since I'm not allowed to speak to him and he cannot come out here. I'd best go hunt up some supper or Damion will know I didn't do it this morning."

Ma held up the glass for her to drink. "That is the trouble with being the best. No one believes you when you have a bad day."

Kitty drank the sweet and sour liquid, then set the glass down on the table. "You'll be all right while I'm gone?"

"I was this morning. I keep Daniel with me when you're gone. For some reason, Damion isn't as liable to blow up with the boy close by. I use that to my advantage."

"Hello? Is anyone home?" Hannah's happy voice came from the front yard.

"Gracious, I didn't even hear the car drive up." Ma paled slightly. "That could've been very bad for me."

Kitty went to the door and opened it wide, admitting her friend. "I didn't expect you, especially not all the way out here." Kitty glanced behind Hannah since Damion could come from anywhere.

"I brought this." Hannah held up a large basket, inside of which was a covered copper pan. "Blake will join us later, but he had to head right back to town. I'd wanted to talk to you anyway, but after seeing what I saw, I thought it was important that I come out early. What I saw isn't fit to discuss over the supper table." She tugged her hat from her head and pressed her hairpins back in place.

Ma took the pan from her hands. "Thank you. I hope the drive wasn't too uncomfortable. It's been unseasonably cool this year."

"Blake wouldn't dream of leaving the house without at least three blankets for me. He makes certain I never catch a chill."

Kitty poured Hannah some of the lemonade from the pitcher and pulled out a chair for her. Hannah took a seat and sighed softly. "First, I want you to know that Mr. Easton has hired Mac to look for your father."

Kitty felt her jaw go slack, but there was little she could do about it. Why would Thad do all these things if he didn't care? Yet how could she witness what she had and not believe he didn't care for Nancy? "Searching for my father?" she asked.

"Yes. It's only been a few days, but Mac has already been to the last known place where your father was supposed to have gone, and they don't recall him being there within the last year. And since he was such a memorable man, it's unlikely they just wouldn't remember. Mac's asking around with a few of your father's known acquaintances, but the leads aren't giving him any new information."

All of Kitty's family had assumed Pa was dead. Though, as dangerous as his work was, Kitty had always presumed he'd be killed by an animal. Perhaps he had, though she hadn't found him on his trap line.

"Interestingly, Mac wasn't the first one to go asking about Aspen Horwath," Hannah continued. "Apparently, a large gentleman too well-dressed to be taken seriously asked if he'd been seen about a month ago."

"Damion?" Ma asked. "Why would he go to a den of thieves to ask about his brother? He's the only one I can think of who would, and the only well-dressed man who had any reason to look for Aspen."

"It is interesting but doesn't tell us anything new. We all assumed Pa wouldn't be coming home." Kitty squeezed Ma's shoulder to lessen the blow.

"I'm sorry, Kitty. I know he wasn't a kind man to any of you, but he did provide as best he could. I can see that here. The house is comfortable." Hannah glanced around the tidy kitchen.

Kitty stifled her defense of Thad—he'd been the one to make it comfortable of late. "Was that what you came out to tell us? I can see why you wouldn't want to share that in front of the boys."

"That's not all." Hannah sucked in a deep breath. "The rules and prizes in the shooting competition have changed. Now as a prize for the winner of the women's competition, the winner will receive a paid luncheon with Thad Easton, the most eligible bachelor in town. There was such a line to enter the contest we couldn't get near the signup sheet. They closed the line before Blake could sign up. You'll have to shoot in my place for the women's and I don't know how we'll get you in the elite."

"Signed up? Blake was going to shoot?" Kitty couldn't hide her surprise. The man never wanted anyone to know just how good he was, though Hannah bragged about her husband often.

"Yes...in the elite competition. There were only three people signed up, and he thought four would make it more sporting. But what he'd really hoped to accomplish was to make sure that you would have someone to compete against, so you wouldn't forfeit by lack of contenders." Hannah glanced out the window. "But my concern is with the women's."

Kitty released her death grip on her lemonade glass before she broke it. There wasn't an extra dollar to sign up for the women's competition. No matter how much she'd like to best Nancy Powers. A soft voice in the back of her mind reminded her that her thoughts were prideful, but they also lessened the sting.

"If I were shooting, I'd make sure Thad didn't have to have luncheon with anyone. But I won't be here to collect the prize." Though Kitty would like to. The mere idea of what people would say about her going to lunch with Thad made her want to giggle.

"Will your uncle let you be there? I'll let you shoot in my place. I only entered because I thought it would be fun to compete with you. I didn't expect to win, and I don't need the prize."

"You wanted to compete with me?" That surprised Kitty. Most people avoided shooting against her, leaving her feeling unsure whether she was just good or people simply didn't want to be near her.

Hannah grinned. "Sure, you're the only woman I've met who could hit the head of a nickel at twenty paces. If I could even get close, I'd be proud of the accomplishment."

"With Damion's decision that you can't see Thad, I wonder if he'll still allow you to shoot in the contest. I know he wants to see how capable you are, but it's a risk. Damion Horwath isn't a gambling man." Ma drummed her fingers on the table. "He might not make a decision until that day. Go to the competition or leave town, those will be our options."

Kitty's stomach twisted. She could lose her chance to win and to say goodbye.

"What if we brought Blake in on this little plan, and he arrived to take you to the competition? Perhaps the plan we tell your uncle will be to get us there in style. Your uncle isn't going to say no to a former Pinkerton and deputy."

"I don't think he's a fool, but he might try to find a way around it." Ma winced.

"We'll leave the explanations and plans up to my husband. Trust me when I tell you the man can think on his feet. He really was a great agent."

"You worked with him on a case, didn't you say that?" Kitty had wondered how the two had met, but Hannah was always somewhat evasive about that part of her life.

"Once, but that was in the past, and I have no interest in pretending or investigating now. The only secret plans I want to make now are how to corner my husband in the evening before he gets too comfortable in his chair after supper."

Ma giggled softly. "Men do like their relaxation after a meal."

Kitty sat back from the conversation having nothing to add. She didn't have a husband, nor would she if Damion had his way. Even if she won the competition, it meant nothing now. He'd take her winnings and they'd disappear.

Unfortunately, she wasn't even sure Thad would miss her now. She stood from her seat and went to the window under the guise of watching for her uncle. "If Blake can come, I'll play my part as well as I can. It might be the last chance I get to see you for a long time."

She watched as Blake pulled into the driveway, and Damion sat next to him in the car. He must have met up with Blake in town and asked for a ride home.

"We won't let that happen, Kitty," Hannah muttered. "We'll find a way."

She'd trusted Thad to find a way too, but all she'd gotten was hurt.

19

"You going to come out here and help me?" Jack said, eyeing Thad from the door. Just beyond him, Thad could see a crowd milling about, talking loudly. Not a one of them was at the lumberyard to buy anything.

They'd been coming for the last two days, either expressing interest in the newest prize for the shooting contest or laughing at him. He'd spent his entire adult life avoiding laughter after having been teased mercilessly as the only child of a man who stuttered. A man who was brilliant, but who never made his mark in the world because of his fear of people judging him for his inability to speak perfectly.

Thad pushed to his feet and came to the door. Three women pressed Jack back into him in their exuberance. "I've signed up. If I win, we can sit at the table in the far corner. It's quiet there," one woman said.

"Don't start sending your wedding invitations yet, Mary. Any one of us could win," another woman said.

Nancy stood next to Mr. Slade near the front, both of them surveying the crowd with gleams in their eyes.

"Mr. Easton!" Mr. Slade waved him over. "I meant to congratulate you. Your idea to offer such a generous prize has more than quadrupled the number of entrants for the women's competition." He thrust the paper at Thad.

He took a quick glance down the sheet and noticed that Kitty's name had been crossed out. "What happened to Kitty's entry?"

Mr. Slade snorted. "I changed my mind. She wasn't needed to build excitement. Not only did we sell almost thirty more entries, the number of tickets to attend the competition is already almost double last year. We'll have money left over if we're careful."

"This was not my idea, and I won't accept the blame for it," Thad said.

Cecil shoved his way through the door of the lumberyard and looked lost in the sea of people. He craned his neck and stood on tiptoe until he saw Thad, then made his way over. "What in tarnation is going on in here?"

"A celebration, Cecil. We are celebrating the success of this year's shooting contest." Mr. Slade pounded Cecil on the back.

"We haven't even had the competition yet," the older man groused.

"Yes, but we have so much interest, there's no question we'll be able to build the roller-skating rink, which was the goal all along," Mr. Slade replied. Though the way he stared at Thad made Thad wonder if that were truly the case.

Cecil glared at the banker. "It isn't right, putting a man on display like he's one of the bawdy girls you try so hard to hide. It's six of one and half a dozen of the other. You should be ashamed."

Thad's reactions froze. He wasn't sure what to say. Cecil was right, but he'd never seen anyone question Mr. Slade or anyone else in a similar position.

Mr. Slade snorted. "I'm sure you'll enjoy the rink enough, or at least the amount of money it brings to your store when people stop by on their way out of town. You won't complain when it pads your profit."

"I will complain. If the gains are ill-gotten, they'll reap what was sown. Money isn't everything. It isn't even most of the things. It's simply a means to an end. I won't be donating to the competition next year. I'm sorry, Thad. You work hard to make this contest something the town can be proud of, but this year, it stinks too much of things I'd rather this town move away from." He tugged his wool hat off his head and crushed it in his hands. "Feels like walking backwards. That's all I came in here to say."

For once, Mr. Slade was silent. Thad stepped forward and clapped Cecil on the shoulder. "You have to do what is good for your conscience. I won't ask you next year." He wondered how many other people who donated this year wouldn't after Mr. Slade had made a circus of the event.

The unease in the room soon had people filtering back out into the street, leaving Thad and Jack to sweep up the mess left behind. Jack grabbed the big metal dustpan off the wall and held it for Thad. "Do you think this will doom the contest for next year?"

Thad had known the contests couldn't go on forever. At some point he would have to either pass on the work or the town would want to stop. He secretly hoped that the rowdy gambling town built on mining would calm into a regular city, and a shooting competition wouldn't seem right anymore. "I don't know. I can't predict the future."

He'd hoped Katherine was in his future, but after two days of seeing no sign of her or her family, he had to wonder if Damion had merely whisked them out of town without anyone the wiser. "Have you been out to see Katherine?"

Jack snorted softly. "I see where your mind is when it should be on your business. You've got to think about how all this will affect you here. If Cecil is upset, he's repeating what he's heard at his store. Others are bothered by what Mr. Slade is doing."

A cloud of dust rose between them as Thad swept the pile of dirt into the dustpan. For a town with paved streets, the townspeople had tracked a lot of dirt in. There was only so long he could stall Jack though. His question, of whether the contest might be doomed, was one that deserved an answer, if he had one.

"I can't help but be concerned. Katherine's uncle threatened to take her away if he so much as got wind of any plot to stop him from taking his brother's family into what would amount to slavery."

Jack slowly rose and dumped the dust in the bin, then hung the pan on the nail above it. "I would be distracted, too. I am, to be honest. The reason Kitty and I get along so well is because her brother is one of my closest friends. As close as one can be after I left school and he didn't, that is."

"Alex might not be able to stay a friend much longer."

Jack reached for the broom and took it over to the corner. "What's your plan? You obviously have one. I want to help. There's lots of us who'd help."

"I think the only way to get them free for sure is to have Damion arrested for killing his brother. He as much as admitted to me that he'd done it."

"That won't mean anything. He'll say you're lying." Jack leaned against the high table they used to look over blueprints and tilted his head. "The one thing that people with money seem to value the most is other people with money. Their opinions matter more than almost anything else. Kitty told me once that's why wealth could be a sin. It's not because there's actual sin in the money, but what it does to the way you treat people. When you think you're pretty important, you can't make God important."

"You can't serve two masters…" He'd heard that his entire life, but he'd always assumed he could and would be different. Why shouldn't he seek wealth and position? Except for the past two weeks he'd been afraid of admitting how he felt about Katherine, ashamed others might not agree with his choice.

"You're right. They do," Thad continued. "And with that, I think I know just exactly how to make sure Kitty is protected along with her family. I need you to do something for me though." He dug a coin from his pocket and handed it to Jack. "I need you to ride to Belle Fourche. Take your time. You might end up staying there overnight, but you can stay with the deputy and his wife. I need you to tell them to come early tomorrow and that I'll need to know everything about what Mac found."

Jack tilted his head and narrowed his eyes. "I can do that, but it seems like a waste of my time. Shouldn't I be here helping you?"

Thad doubted there would be much left of his business within forty-eight hours, so helping wasn't necessary. "I'll pay you for as long as I can, but this is the most important thing right now." He'd also have to hire someone else to make sure Katherine and her family were still living in their house outside of town. He couldn't risk going himself.

Jack clutched the coin. "All right. I'll do that."

"I'll pay you more when you return. Come tonight if they are willing to drive tonight."

Jack gave a firm nod and dashed out into the street. For once, he didn't look around. His purpose was singular.

Within seconds, the door to the lumberyard

opened again, and Mr. Powers brushed dust from his long black coat. He was perfectly tailored from the top of his hat to the tip of his boots, not a thread out of place.

"Mr. Easton, a word with you please?" He headed right for Thad's office as if it were his own. If Nancy had her way, that could be a possibility.

Thad followed Mr. Powers in and closed the door, slightly surprised the man hadn't gone all the way behind the desk. Instead, he sat in the chair, balancing his hat on his knee.

"Can I offer you something to drink?" Not that Thad had anything right there available, but it seemed like the most appropriate thing to do.

"No, thank you. I'll cut right to the chase. My daughter sent me an urgent message four days ago that an offer of marriage was imminent, and I needed to return home posthaste." He spun his hat on his knee slowly. "Do you know anything about that?"

Thad knew everyone had plotted his life without his say, mostly because he'd kept silent when he shouldn't have. All in the name of looking respectful and responsible. "No sir. I don't see Miss Powers often and don't know about her marital situation."

Mr. Powers chuckled, though it was humorless. "I suspected as much. I'm growing tired of emotional tantrums and demands. It's time someone else managed them. I'd offer you the job, but I very much need you to remain my steadfast partner. I fear my daughter is spoiled and, just like a soft apple put in a barrel full of unspoiled ones will rot the whole container, my daughter would ruin the solid partnership we have. That is, in fact, why I stopped by. Should you have been the one to offer marriage, I was…going to attempt to talk you out of it, sorry to say."

Chuckling at the situation would sour things, so Thad kept his feelings to himself other than offering thanks. "She seems to be spending quite a bit of time with Mr. Slade from the bank, though he's much older than she is," Thad noted.

Mr. Powers slowly nodded his head. "That would be a partnership I could manage, especially since I don't bank here in Deadwood anymore, though my wife does." He snorted. "If choosing in this manner would keep my wife from spending so much money, I may solve two problems in one." He slowly stood and offered his hand to Thad. "I'm glad we were able to get this squared away so quickly. You've always been a man I could trust. Don't change." He fit his hat back atop his head and left with a nod.

Thad had every intention of changing—for the better—and hoped he'd still have his business to work with Mr. Powers in the future. The fact was that Katherine was more important to him than his business, and he should've realized that from the start. He could've saved her earlier if he'd simply brushed aside her concerns about what people would think of him—concerns he'd thought justified his own worries. If he'd told her he put her above his concerns about what others thought, she might have married him when he'd asked.

He braced his hands on the desk and lowered his head, giving himself time to pray about what he had to do. After years of relying on himself, he'd need strength from God to make it through the next day.

20

The day of the contest had finally arrived, and Thad's stomach was as tight as a sailor's knot. He'd already spoken to the county assessor about his plan and said another prayer that it would work out. If Katherine wasn't there, he'd lose his business and his heart all in the same day.

But he'd go after Katherine with more fervor than he'd given his business. He wouldn't lose her.

"Good morning, Thad." Blake Longfellow strode toward him with Mac on one side and his wife, Hannah, on the other. Jack had returned to Deadwood with them the night before, giving them time to plan ahead. Just behind Hannah was a person dressed in fine clothes with her blond hair up and a beguiling new Stetson to cap it off; she was wearing a kerchief across her face, but he'd know her anywhere.

What he hoped was that no one else would. "Good morning. This must be your sister…" He tried to remember the name Hannah had told him, the one Katherine would use all day to hide from her uncle.

"Alice. This is my sister Alice." Hannah motioned the woman forward.

The moment their eyes met, he knew Katherine was hurting over something, but he couldn't ask what. The dark pools of her eyes asked him a hundred questions he couldn't answer with so many people around.

"My sister is going to take my place today. She's a much better shot than I am." Hannah laughed. "Is that all right, Mr. Easton?"

"Yes, that's fine. Thank you." He didn't mean to brush Hannah away, but he wanted to know what was wrong with Katherine and how he could fix the situation.

Mac approached and lowered his voice. "I've spoken to the sheriff and made him aware of the situation. He told me that he couldn't make a case until they found the body. He didn't much appreciate it when I asked if he wanted it in his office."

Katherine visibly paled, and Thad reached out to touch her arm. She yanked it from his reach and stepped back.

Hannah frowned and glanced between the two of them. "She's a little shy since she heard her beau was interested in another woman. She caught them holding hands when they thought she wasn't looking. Now she doesn't like to be near men at all."

Thad hated the subterfuge. Was Hannah speaking of her real sister or of Katherine…or about him? Had Katherine witnessed him and Nancy in the street when he'd been trying, again, to save himself the strain of standing up for himself?

"That is a low and cowardly thing to do. I'm sorry to hear it." He looked Katherine in the eyes. "Sometimes situations aren't what they seem, or at least, they aren't completely what they seem."

Jack shot off a starting pistol near the first target, signaling the start of the competition. Katherine carried over the dark wooden case that Thad recognized as holding the pink pistol he'd purchased for her. She got in line to take her shot and waited until the end. Since she was a last-minute change, she had to shoot last.

Damion pushed his way to the front of the crowd. "Where is Kitty Horwath? She was supposed to be shooting today. Where did she go?" He mopped the sweat pouring down his temples.

At least the disguise of a wealthy dress and mask seemed enough to fool Damion. Thad had worried it wouldn't since Thad had recognized her easily.

"Sir, I'll ask that you do not disturb our shooter," Thad said.

"You!" Damion pointed first to Thad, then at Hannah who stood behind Kitty. "You two are in league with each other, but you won't win."

The crowd started mumbling for him to be quiet and let the last woman shoot. As of now, Nancy was in the lead. She waited under the cover of a broad tent to keep the sun off her face. Thad couldn't make himself look back there. She'd given him a possessive glance right after her shot, making him suspect her father had not gotten through to her about Mr. Slade.

Katherine, known to the crowd as Alice, stepped to the line. She had the charisma of a tiger. She knew she could win easily, and this wouldn't be a challenge for her. She raised the pistol to the level of her hip and took a shot without even aligning the sights.

A notch appeared on the target that hadn't been there before. Dead center. No question about the winner. The crowd erupted as Jack raced the thirty yards down range to look at what was obvious. He confirmed the shot, then over the next few minutes let her take her other four shots, each one enlarging the gouge in the center of the target.

By the end, the crowd was ready to make Alice their mayor. As usual, without speaking at all, or visibly showboating, she'd managed to enthrall the crowd by doing what she loved to do and did well.

Thad raised his hands to silence the crowd.

"Alice wins the prize for the women's competition. Can you come up to the podium?"

Katherine hesitated slightly and glanced over her shoulder toward the crowd. Thad laid a protective hand on her back and spoke through his teeth so no one could read his lips. "Trust me." He loved that she immediately relaxed beneath his fingers.

He led her up to the podium. "Alice Douglas is the winner of the women's competition. Congratulations."

Blake yelled from the crowd to egg them on. "Let her shoot in the elite! She's good enough." The crowd soon joined in the chant. Had they been told ahead of time that a woman would compete, they wouldn't have allowed it. But because Katherine looked like a person who belonged there, they didn't argue the matter. How had he been so blind?

Thad held up his hands. "I'll let Alice compete in the elite competition because one of our shooters didn't show up. I've also increased the prize. The winner of the elite competition…" He swallowed hard. "The winner will take over ownership of the lumberyard."

Katherine gasped next to him on the pedestal. He ducked his head slightly to lead her off. "Do you trust me?"

With an ever so slight nod of her head, she calmed his racing heart.

KITTY HELD HERSELF IN PLACE, no matter that she'd like to run. Uncle Damion stood just a few feet away, glaring at her as if he might suspect who she was. Maybe he did, but there was little he could do in front of everyone. Unfortunately, she knew her brothers and Ma were locked back at home, preventing her from doing anything rash.

Damion had allowed her to go the night before when Hannah and Blake had arrived to take her into town for the contest. Only when Blake showed his badge did Damion allow her to go with them, though. Now that the competition had begun, Damion had to know something was going on.

Kitty glanced over to the large tent where Nancy fumed after losing her chance to have lunch with Thad. Between the threat of Uncle Damion and that of Nancy, she wasn't sure which was worse.

Focusing on the men's competition didn't distract her much. The men were all equally matched, and little changed between contestants. An hour later, the winner of the men's competition was awarded, and he was given the same opportunity as Alice: to win the elite prizes including ownership of the lumberyard.

Kitty had tried to figure out Thad's reasoning for putting his business up as a prize, but nothing she could come up with made any sense. His business meant everything to him. Without it, he wouldn't have the ability to help so many people. How could he simply give it away?

She'd just have to win it to give it back to him. It would be her only way to tell him how she felt before she left.

Thad called a break. While the contestants and crowd were eating on the grass, Mac approached with the Deadwood sheriff at his side. Kitty had met both of them the evening before after Blake and Hannah had picked her up.

"Afternoon." Mac tipped his hat to her. "I didn't believe it until Blake told me. That's a fine disguise." He kept his voice low. "I'll need to speak to you after the event. Some things have come to light regarding your uncle. I want you to know we've already sent men out, and your family is safe. Blake and I will be here until the end of the competition."

"He carries a gun under his coat. Be careful when you arrest him," Kitty said. She could hardly believe what she'd heard over the last day. She'd known Damion was evil and greedy, but she'd never thought he could commit murder to get what he wanted.

Mac glanced around them and lowered his voice, "We'll be apprehending him when he goes back out to the house to gather your family. There's less chance of anyone else being injured in the process that way."

She was glad they'd told her. Otherwise she would've assumed her uncle had gotten away with everything. Within minutes, Jack again shot the starter pistol, and the four entrants—Thad, Amos, Kitty, and the winner of the men's competition—went to the final target.

Kitty knew there would be tension shooting against men. They wouldn't like losing to a woman any more than she would like missing any target. Anytime pride was involved, people got hurt. She stood back, away from the gun rest, letting the first set of men go first.

Thad stood back near her, and she welcomed his presence. Knowing he was there in case something happened with her uncle or in case one of the men became angry calmed her soul. She didn't want to give herself away and inch too close to him, but she wanted to know what he'd meant when he'd said things weren't always what they seemed. She found it strange that his words had echoed those Ma had said about Pa.

Jack ushered her to her spot on the table at the line.

All weapons had to lie on the table in front of each competitor and had to be inspected by one of the judges. Each pistol had to be loaded by one of the judges to check both the weapon and the ammunition used to ensure the contest was fair.

Kitty realized a flaw in her plan at that moment. All the other contestants had a pistol and long gun of various sizes, which she didn't have. Her gun from home, had she brought it, would've given away who she was immediately. Shooting with someone else's weapon would put her at a disadvantage. She knew her own weapons and how she had to adjust the sight on each to hit the target.

Kitty glanced at the judge as he made his way down the table. He would be to her soon. A snide voice behind her mocked her. "Forget something important? I guess you didn't plan to win," Nancy snickered.

Her pistols were fine, but she would need a long gun to compete with the men for the longer distance shots. "Mrs. Douglas?" the judge called to her.

"Yes." Kitty stepped forward, unsure what she should do. If she couldn't compete, Thad would have to win to keep his business.

"She can use mine." Hannah stepped forward and laid a long case on the table.

"Thank you," Kitty whispered, still unsure how she would fare with an unfamiliar weapon.

Amos and the men's winner had shot at the same time, leaving her to shoot at the same time as Thad. How would he handle competing against her? He turned to send a grin her way as if he knew exactly what she was thinking. And that was precisely why she loved him.

Wait... Her hand gripped the pearl-handled pistol, and the judge glared at her for going near it. Loved? She loved him?

"Next up!" the judge called, breaking her from her thoughts.

She had to shoot at a target after that discovery? Her mouth dropped open, tugging the bandana below her nose. Nancy took that moment to grab her arm and yank the fabric down.

"I knew it! You're that no-good Kitty Horwath. You think you're better than everyone else. You have to hide who you are just so people will cheer for you."

She felt more than saw Damion head toward her, and in the next instant, she was tugged to Thad's side. "Enough, get back in the tent. It's not safe for you to be beyond that line, and I won't get accused of cheating just because you're jealous," Thad said to Nancy.

Nancy's mouth dropped open, and her eyes narrowed with hatred. "Jealous? Of *her*?"

Movement to Kitty's right distracted her from Nancy's vitriol as Mac grabbed Uncle Damion from behind and twisted his arm, forcing him to stop. He dug metal cuffs out from a large leather pocket hanging from his belt and soon had Damion under arrest and headed toward the jail.

"Looks like all that's left is to make sure we win my business," Thad murmured next to her.

"Why did you do that? Put your business on the line? I don't understand."

Thad touched her cheek, seemingly unaware of the onlookers. Her heart skipped as she looked around at the shocked faces.

"It was a failsafe. I knew you'd win if saving someone else was your target. Your uncle wouldn't be able to take you if you owned a business, one with a house attached to it. He could no longer claim that you needed him. You would've had a business of your own and a way to care for your family."

"And now you put me in the position of letting you win so you keep it…"

"Or beating me and letting me join you." He grinned.

Her heart filled at the idea that he thought they were equals. He trusted her with his business and his heart. She stepped to the line and suddenly the pressure was gone. She only had to hit the targets. The most important target had already been a bullseye.

What do you know, Annie Oakley's pistol prediction was right.

When the smoke cleared, Kitty had won by fractions of an inch. A car drove up to the edge of the crowd, and her mother and four brothers poured out, racing toward her. They surrounded her, pulling her into a tearful embrace. She may have even indulged in a few tears of her own.

"So, what do you say, Katherine Horwath? You own the lumberyard now." Thad leaned against the aiming table, waiting for her word.

"I think you should keep it. But I'd sure like to join you."

"I can't imagine a better business—and life—partner. Join me?"

She nodded. "I think you know me well enough to call me Kitty now."

He grinned and in the next instant kissed her, right there in front of her ma, brothers, and a crowd of all the people she'd been worried about just minutes before. He deepened the kiss ever so slightly, and for the first time in her life, her knees went weak. She'd never understood how that could happen until Thad.

The crowd whooped a cheer, and Thad pulled away just enough to look her in the eyes. "I love you, Kitty."

She hadn't thought she'd ever get to say the words, but now couldn't wait to say them. "I love you too, Thad."

Epilogue

Nine months later

"I understand what the letter says, but I don't see why you have to give it away. I gave it to you." Thad wrapped his arms around in front of her, pulling her flush with him where they stood at their new dining room table, his body solid against her back.

She took out a pencil and filled in their names, then her own description of how they met: *Kitty Horwath married Thad Easton this 25th of December, 1910, year of our Lord. A competition in Deadwood pitted us against each other, but a last-minute challenge and a test of faith won my heart (and the prize).*

"I know just where to leave it." She wasn't going to challenge the little paper. While her faith was in God, maybe He had worked through the pistol to bring her to Thad, or him to her, or however it had worked. She wasn't going to deny someone else and risk losing her love. In that same way, she'd had an idea last night where the pistol belonged.

"Where?" Thad nuzzled her ear, distracting her.

"The pistol originally belonged to Annie Oakley, and she was part of what was basically a circus." And if Thad would release his hold on her—though only for a short time—she would take it back to the circus.

"So, you're going to take it to the traveling circus just outside of town? I hope they leave soon, or they'll be trapped by the snow."

"Maybe they're waiting for me to drop this off. Then they can move along."

Thad kissed her behind the ear, then squeezed her shoulders. "It's yours to do with as you like. I hope it finds its way into good hands."

She touched the smooth dark wood of the case. When she'd received it, that had been the nicest thing she'd ever owned. Now Thad provided anything she could ever want, especially since all she really wanted was him. They worked hard together at the lumberyard, and feelings toward her family were slowly changing. Now if only she could get her brothers to someday settle down, the cloud over her family name might be erased for good.

Damion had gone to prison for her father's murder, and since she was his next of kin, she had been given the right to manage his accounts. She wouldn't do him wrong, but she wasn't about to make him richer, either. Ma had wanted to stay in her house with the boys, and the first thing Kitty had done was to sign the deed over to Ma. The home had no liens against it, and the money Pa had been paying all those years was only to make Damion richer.

Kitty slid the case into her satchel and slung it over her shoulder. "It will find the perfect hands, I have no doubt about it."

Dear Reader,

I feel like I need to say a few things about Deadwood and this story. As far as I know, I couldn't find any record of a mill in Deadwood; there may have been one, but I can't say so with certainty. However, I needed someone who could provide the supplies necessary for not only the shooting competition, but the new roller rink.

Which brings me to issues number two and three: while a mill in Deadwood is plausible, there is no record of a shooting competition or a roller rink in Deadwood (though there were in other nearby cities). A roller-skating rink would've provided great fun for young and old in Deadwood, but no such place was ever there.

While the town is set up just as I talk about in the story, with Deadwood being in a low gulch with high areas on each end and a flat, grassy area outside of town where the Lodge at Deadwood is now, there was never (as far as I could find) a shooting competition held there. All this is to say, this book is wholly fiction, and I hope you enjoyed it.

I am considering writing a series featuring Kitty's brothers. Be sure to email and let me know if that interests you at Kari@KariTrumbo.com.

Be sure you turn the page and read the first scene in Winnie Griggs' *Disarming His Heart*, book 8 in the Pink Pistol Sisterhood!

Kari

DISARMING HIS HEART

By Winnie Griggs

CHAPTER TWENTY-ONE

CHAPTER 1

Larkin, Missouri, June 1911

Violet Taylor sat in the storeroom of Adeline's Fashion Emporium trying not to bite the fingernails on her good hand. It was a bad habit, one she'd worked hard to overcome.

But when she was really anxious, like now, the urge came creeping back. Violet shifted, adjusting the fit of the sling she wore around her neck. She could hear the murmur of voices on the other side of the storeroom door. But neither voice was Lily's. One of the voice's was Adeline's and the other must be a customer.

After seven months it was still hard to think of the dress shop owner as Aunt Adeline. The seamstress was more Lily's aunt than hers. Although since she and Lily were twins it meant Adeline Clemmons was related to her as well.

The ringing of the shop bell alerted her that the shop door had opened. Was someone leaving or entering? A moment later she heard the unmistakable sound of Lily's breezy voice greeting her aunt.

Violet's stomach fluttered and she stood, no longer able to sit still. No matter how much Wyatt said this plan of his was going to work, she still wasn't sure asking Lily to do this for her was the right thing.

A few minutes later her sister entered the storeroom.

And halted on the threshold.

"Violet! Oh goodness, you're hurt." Lily quickly closed the door behind her. "What happened and how bad is it?"

Violet envied the presence her sister had. The two of them might be identical twins but Lily merely had to enter a room to instantly draw all eyes to herself—and it was all the more remarkable because she seemed completely unaware she had that effect. Violet, on the other hand, was a wallflower, easily

. . .

OVERLOOKED AND DISMISSED.

But Lily was still studying her in some concern so Violet brought her thoughts back to the current situation and raised her right arm, sling and all. "It's not serious, just a sprain. But it's actually the reason we're here."

Before she finished talking the back door opened and Wyatt stepped inside to join them. Wyatt Gleason had been a part of Violet's life for almost as long as she could remember. He was her best friend and her confidant. They looked after each other—in short he was like a big brother to her.

But Lily cast him an accusatory glance. "You didn't tell me she was hurt."

He shrugged and crossed his arms. "I thought it best to save all explanations until we could speak freely."

Violet didn't understand the friction that crackled between Wyatt and Lily on the few occasions they'd been together. Somehow the two of them had gotten off on the wrong foot from the very beginning. Which didn't make sense as it was Wyatt who'd managed to track down Lily and Aunt Adeline and reunite the three of them.

But now was not the time to ponder that so she quickly grabbed the conversational reins again. "I sprained my wrist two days ago." She took her seat again. "Doc said if I ever want to shoot with any degree of accuracy again then I have to wear this sling for at least four weeks." Which was a serious consideration since she made her living performing as a sharpshooter with a traveling show.

Lily finished crossing the room and touched Violet's uninjured arm. "I'm so sorry. Regardless of what

you said this does sound serious. But it's not the end of the world. If you do like the doctor said The

Masked Marvel will be awing the crowds with her skill again in no time."

The Masked Marvel was the name Violet used when she performed her sharpshooter routine. It came

from the fact that she wore a mask and kept her identity secret.

Violet grimaced as she sat again and slid over on the bench to make room for her sister. "I agree. But

it's not quite that simple."

Lily arranged her skirts as she sat. "Why not?"

"The Masked Marvel is a big draw for the circus." She usually spoke of her circus act identity in the

third person. "She needs to make an appearance whether she performs her act or not. She'll ride in the

opening parade and maybe walk through the crowds a time or two."

Lily didn't seem convinced. "So you just add the sling to your costume for the next month." She

waved a hand airily. "It'll just make you seem all the more dangerous and mysterious."

Surely that wasn't a touch of envy in Lily's voice? "But if the Masked Marvel and Violet Taylor both appear with slings at the same time it won't take long for people to start figuring out they're the same person."

"Oh. I see." Lily's expression took on a thoughtful cast. Then she smiled brightly. "Well then, you get someone to pretend to be the Masked Marvel without the sling."

It was Wyatt who answered this time. "Good idea. But it won't work for two reasons. One, the accident happened while she was in costume so lots of people know the Masked Marvel was injured. And two, even if that wasn't the case, if the Masked Marvel isn't injured, then whoever is wearing the costume would be expected to shoot."

Lily grimaced. "I'm sorry, you've obviously already thought this out before you came here." She turned back to Violet. "You said you need my help—what can I do?"

Violet shared a look with Wyatt, wondering how to ask such a big favor of the sister she'd only reconnected with seven months ago. For a moment neither of them spoke.

In the meantime, the storeroom door opened again and Aunt Adeline walked in, leaving the door slightly ajar behind her. "Mrs. Givens finally left and I put a "Gone to Lunch" sign on the door so we can have some privacy." She looked from one to the other of them. "So what did I miss?"

Adeline Clemmons was a petite, white-haired woman with a charming smile and grandmotherly demeanor. But Violet could sense an unexpected inner strength and determination in her. Based on her appearance she could be any age from forty-five to sixty-five. And though Lily called her Aunt Adeline she was really their great-aunt, the sister of their grandmother.

It was Lily who answered her question. "You haven't missed much. Vi and Wyatt were just about to ask me a favor." She turned to Violet with an impatient toss of her head. "Oh, for goodness sake, Vi, whatever it is just ask."

Violet stood and gave Adeline her seat. Then she took a deep breath, locked gazes with Lily and blurted out her request. "I want you to swap places with me."

Lily sat up straighter. "What?"

Violet saw their aunt put a gentle hand on Lily's skirt. But she kept her focus on her twin. It was so important that she make Lily understand. "I know it's a lot to ask but it would only be for a few weeks."

Violet resolutely held her sister's gaze. "It's the perfect solution, the only solution really. You can wear the sling when you're in costume so no one will expect you to do any shooting. And when you're being just plain old Violet you can use your arm freely.

It'll also have the added benefit of completely throwing

off any suspicions."

"But I can't just drop everything and head off to whatever town your circus is parked in. I have

responsibilities here." She waved toward her aunt. "I can't ask Aunt Adeline to run this place on her

own."

But their aunt blithely waved off that concern. "Don't let me hold you back. I can keep this place

running on my own if it's just for a few weeks"

Violet shot a quick, grateful smile her aunt's way then turned back to Lily. "She wouldn't have to.

While you're pretending to be me, I'll be right here pretending to be you." She grimaced self-consciously.

"I know I don't have your fashion expertise but I can help in other ways." She cast a rather shy glance at

the lady sitting beside Lily. "And it'll give me a chance to get to know Aunt Adeline a bit better."

Her aunt's expression softened. "I'd like that as well, my dear. We've lost so many years."

That seemed to give Lily pause. "If I agree to do this," she said slowly, then held up a hand. "And I'm

not yet convinced I should. But if I do, what would I need to do?"

Some of the tension eased from Violet's shoulders. She hadn't been at all certain Lily would agree to

the plan, but at least she seemed willing to consider it.

"Nothing too difficult. You would wear the

Masked Marvel costume to make an appearance in any

PARADES when the circus arrives in a new town and at the opening of the show. But my act won't be

performed until my arm is healed so you won't have to handle any firearms."

"Good." While Violet was an expert marksman it was no secret that Lily absolutely refused to even

hold a gun. Not due to any moral or societal constraints, but because they terrified her. "And what about

when I'm not in costume?"

"I have some other minor duties with the circus that you'll be expected to take care of—Wyatt can

make sure you know all the wheres, whens and hows. Otherwise, your time is your own. And you would

live in my wagon—it's not very large, but it's comfortable and private."

Lily nodded then turned to her aunt. "What about you? Do you truly think you can manage the shop

on your own for a month?" She glanced her sister's way. "No offense but I don't think you know much

about fabrics and trims, not to mention taking measurements and making alternations."

Aunt Adeline jumped in before Violet could respond. "We'll be just fine. I'm sure Violet is a quick

study. Besides, many of our customers know just what they want so it's only a matter of taking their

orders. And she'll have her sling as an excuse not to actually do fittings or take measurements or anything
else physical."

Lily turned to Wyatt. "What about you, do you really think we can succeed at fooling everyone?" Her
tone and expression held a note of challenge.

He spread his hands. "Since this was my idea in the first place I'd say I'm solidly on board with the
plan."

She stared at him a moment longer then nodded. "Where is the circus right now?"

"On the way to Texas. We'll be touring several towns over the next few months."

Lily gave a mock pout. "I suppose it was too much to expect some place exciting like New Orleans or
New York." Then she turned serious again and met Violet's gaze. "How soon would this swap need to
take place?"

"The sooner the better. Wyat has train tickets in hand for tomorrow."

"And just how long is a few weeks?"

Violet cupped her right elbow with her left hand. "Doc said it would probably take about four weeks
for my arm to heal properly."

"Oh." Lily managed to infuse a wealth of disappointment in that one syllable.

Did that mean she wasn't going to agree to their plan? "What is it?"

Lily traced a circle on the seat of the bench with her finger. "I've been working with Pastor Carson on a children's program for the church's twenty-fifth anniversary celebration. The performance is scheduled to take place on the twenty-third."

Violet's heart fell. That was just three weeks away. And she knew Lily had formed an attachment for the town's preacher. There was no way she'd want to miss such a big event.

She was just about to tell her sister she understood and would find another way to tackle her problem when Lily straightened.

She gave Violet a determined look. "So you'll not only need to take my place leading the practice sessions but you'll also have to direct the actual performance." Then she grinned. "But you're used to performing in front of crowds so perhaps you'll do a better job of it than I have."

Violet wasn't particularly excited about taking over that aspect of Lily's life, but she was too relieved to worry about that at the moment. "Does that mean you'll do it?"

Her sister nodded. "Of course. I know how much keeping your Masked Marvel identity a secret is to you. And I know you'd do the same for me."

"I truly would. Oh Lily you're so generous to disrupt your life to help me this way."

Lily grinned. "To be honest, a part of me actually looking forward to it. I've barely been outside of Larkin since I moved here as a little girl." She waved a hand. "But you get to travel freely around the country. And almost nightly you receive admiration and accolades from the audiences you perform for."

Violet grimaced. "It's not nearly as glamorous as you make it sound."

Her sister was undeterred. "I guess I'm about to find that out." Then her eyes narrowed slightly as she shot Violet a stern look. "Just make sure you don't let the pastor down—everything has to go perfectly."

"You have my word." Violet gave Lily's hand a squeeze. "I know how much he means to you."

They shared a meaningful smile which was interrupted when Wyatt cleared his throat.

"Now that that's settled, we need to lay out a plan."

Lily wrinkled her nose. "What kind of plan?"

"Like Violet said, you and I will board the train headed to Jefferson, Texas tomorrow to meet up with the circus. I can fill you in on most of what you need to know about living Violet's life during the trip. And I'm certain your Aunt Adeline can do the same for Violet. But I figured you ladies would want to spend what time you have to answer any questions you might have of a more personal nature, things that are likely to come up when you're pretending to be the other."

The sound of someone knocking on the shop door interrupted their conversation.

Aunt Adeline popped up from her seat. "Oh dear, I forgot Edda Rodgers had a twelve-thirty appointment for a fitting." She placed a hand on Lily's shoulder as she started to get up. "You stay right here, I'll take care of her. Or better yet, why don't you take Violet and Wyatt to our quarters upstairs where you'll all be more comfortable. Just give me a few minutes to get Edda into the fitting room." And with that the dressmaker bustled out, carefully closing the door behind her.

As Lily stood she glanced from Violet to Wyatt and back again. "You two have obviously had more time to think this through than I have. What do you see as the obstacles we'll have to overcome? Other than the obvious, of course."

Wyatt raised a brow. "The obvious?"

"Yes. I won't know any of the people in Violet's world and she won't know any of the folks in mine. There are bound to be references in conversations that we don't understand."

Violet nodded. "Yes, well, we're hoping that you'll stay close to Wyatt and I'll stay close to Aunt Adeline so they can help smooth over any of those awkward moments."

"Is there anyone we'll want to let in on our secret?"

"Just a handful. We figured for this to work it would be best to keep the circle as small as possible. Why, do you feel differently?"

"I'm thinking we'll want to let Dr. Matthews know."

. . .

Violet frowned. "Why? I don't expect the arm to give me any trouble."

"You can't be certain of that. But there's another reason. If you walk around town wearing that sling he'll wonder why he wasn't involved in putting it there."

"Oh, that makes sense. Can the good doctor be trusted to keep our secret?"

"He's very discreet." Then Lily's lips curved in a mischievous grin. "Besides, he's a widower and I think he's a bit smitten with Aunt Adeline."

Violet filed that little nugget of insight away as she returned Lily's smile. "Is there anyone else you think will notice anything amiss?"

Her sister seemed to ponder that a moment, then finally shook her head. "You wouldn't be able to fool Gertie of course—she's my best friend and knows me almost better than I know myself. But fortunately she's out of town visiting her sister in St. Louis."

"But will she be gone for the full four weeks?"

"Oh, good question. She's due back the day before the celebration." Lily waved a hand. "But if it becomes necessary to tell her you can do so with the assurance that she's entirely trustworthy." She straightened. "I think we've given Aunt Adeline enough time. Follow me and I'll escort you upstairs."

Books in the Pink Pistol Sisterhood Series

In Her Sights by **Karen Witemeyer**
Book 1 ~ March 30
Love on Target by **Shanna Hatfield**
Book 2 ~ April 10
Love Under Fire by **Cheryl Pierson**
Book 3 ~ April 20
Bulletproof Bride by **Kit Morgan**
Book 4 ~ April 30
Bullseye Bride by **Kari Trumbo**
Book 5 ~ May 10
Disarming His Heart by **Winnie Griggs**
Book 6 ~ May 20
One Shot at Love by **Linda Broday**
Book 7 ~ May 30
Armed & Marvelous by **Pam Crooks**
Book 8 ~ June 10
Lucky Shot by **Shanna Hatfield**
Book 9 ~ June 20
Aiming for His Heart by **Julie Benson**
Book 10 ~ June 30
Pistol Perfect by **Jessie Gussman**
Book 11 ~ July 10

BOOKS IN THE PINK PISTOL SISTERHOOD SERIES

*See all the Pink Pistol Sisterhood Books at
www.petticoatsandpistols.com.*

ABOUT THE AUTHOR

Where western meets happily ever after.

Kari Trumbo is an international bestselling author of historical and contemporary Christian romance and romantic suspense. She loves reading, listening to contemporary Christian music, singing when no one's listening, and curling up near the wood stove when winter hits. She makes her home in central Minnesota—where the trees and lakes are plentiful—with her husband of over twenty years, two daughters, two sons, a few cats, and a bunny who's the star of one of her books.

Want a free book? Just visit me at: https://KariTrumbo.com

facebook.com/karitrumboauthor
instagram.com/karitrumboauthor

Made in the USA
Coppell, TX
07 September 2023

21328304R00121